From Indigo Sea Press
By J. R. Hobeck

Smokestack

The Winter

indigoseapress.com

Smokestack

By

J. R. Hobeck

Abyss Books
Published by Indigo Sea Press
Winston-Salem

Abyss Books
Indigo Sea Press
302 Ricks Drive
Winston-Salem, NC 27103

First Abyss Books edition published
January, 2016
Abyss Books, Moon Sailor and all production design are trademarks of Indigo Sea Press, used under license.

For information regarding bulk purchases of this book, digital purchase and special discounts, please contact the publisher at
indigoseapress.com

Cover design by Tracy Beltran

Manufactured in the United States of America
ISBN 978-1-63066-314-8

"To Jenni. Thank you for not letting this stay a short story."

Chapter 1

Gregg Childress drove the giant gravel truck up the ramp toward the rim of the quarry. As he reached the top of the ramp he was blinded. The sun shining on the dusty windshield created so much glare he could not see. The truck rumbled to a stop. He ran the wipers and watched the washer fluid first streak and smear then clear the windshield. He realized the glare was not getting much better. It dawned on him that the filth on his own glasses was causing most of the problem. He took a handkerchief out of his pocket and began to wipe the accumulated grime from the thick safety lenses.

As he wiped, the weather report came on the radio.

"...Today's high a blistering 94, low tonight expected to only get down to 78 under clear skies. Tomorrow, there is a possibility of thunderstorms in the evening as a cooler front comes through. We certainly could use the rain. Stay tuned for..."

Gregg liked the warm nights of the summer. He often sat in his swimming trunks in the quick set pool he had bought a couple summers ago. He liked to sit out there at night looking at the stars and daydream about being an astronaut. He imagined the hum of the pool filter being the rocket engines propelling him to Mars or Pluto or the jump limit, beyond which he could flip a switch that would propel him to anywhere in the galaxy. That had been his dream as a boy. He had tried to get into the Air Force when he graduated from high school, but had been a little too heavy and had been told that, even if he had gotten in, he would never be a pilot because of his poor eyesight.

He finished wiping his glasses, and was delighted when he put them back on and could see clearly. The rock dust that was omnipresent in the quarry coated everything. The lack of rain lately had made it worse. Even walking with a light tread would raise a cloud of dust. He looked down to the gauges on the truck and noticed that the engine was running a bit hot; not close to the red, but hotter than usual. The radiator needed a good hosing off. He made a mental note to take care of that, and check the air filter at the end of the shift. He drove the truck to the big hopper at the end of the cement plant and dumped the load of limestone. He started the trip back down into the pit to pick up another load.

Slowly turning the switchbacks as he went, he drove the truck down the ramp. He had reached a level plateau, a shelf about fifty yards wide that skirted the perimeter of the active pit. Anywhere active quarrying was being done could be reached from here. He drove along the limestone wall parallel to the road in front of the plant that was about seventy feet above his head. Followed this path around an angled outcropping of stone that had been left in place because it wasn't been considered useful, he turned the corner at the end of the outcropping and headed toward where the bulldozers were filling another truck.

Gregg was about twenty yards from where he would queue up to get his next load when there was a brilliant flash to his right. The truck rumbled for a moment then died. The radio cut out. He looked at the gauges. There were no readings. Even the battery gauge was zero. He turned the key to try and restart the massive diesel. Nothing happened. There was not even so much as a click, a cough or a single whir.

He looked up, and noticed that one of the bulldozers had stopped with its load of stone halfway dumped out into one of the other trucks. The operator was moving levers and nothing was happening.

Then the bulldozer operator looked up. To Greg it appeared the man was looking between two of the dump trucks. The operator's face went pale. He stopped shifting the levers. Slowly, mechanically, he undid his seat belt. His eyes never left what he was staring at.

Gregg looked to his right as well. He could not see what the bulldozer operator was looking at, his view obscured by the back of the cab. He got out of the truck, walked to the front of the truck and stopped dead in his tracks.

Gregg saw a giant object. It had the appearance of the monstrous metal horn of a giant robotic bull that had been thrust, wide end first, into the pit. His first thought was that it was a hallucination. He had forgotten to take his medicine last night and had only taken his regular dose this morning. Then he looked around at the other people in the pit and realized he was not the only one seeing this thing. Despite the fear of what he was seeing, he was glad at least that it was not his mind playing tricks on him. He had learned he could deal with anything in the real world much easier than he could with the things that lurked in the shadowy corners of his mind.

He stood staring at the thing for nearly a full minute before it dawned on him that there might be some of the other employees much closer to that thing. From where he stood, it looked like one end of the object was near where the engineers were setting up for the next blast. He tried to remember the blast schedule, realizing the next scheduled blast was in 2 days. The final inspection of the bore holes would be happening today.

Gregg started to run toward where the next blast would be happening. He wanted to be sure everyone over there was safe. As he ran, he kept an eye the entire time on this thing that had just appeared. Scenes from every science fiction alien movie he had ever seen started to flash though his mind. He kept coming back to the scene in Alien when the alien's ship is first seen. This thing vaguely reminded him of that. When he suddenly had to stop running and vomit, he had an image of one of the alien babies bursting out of his chest. His body gave the closest approximation it could muster, his breakfast bursting forth from his mouth. When he was finished, he wiped his mouth with his handkerchief.

He kept walking, out of breath, toward the blast area. As he got close he called the name of the two people he knew would be doing the inspection.

"Harry. Stephen?. Where are you? Harrrrry?... Steeeeve?" He called.

Gregg kept calling as he walked. He saw the pickup they had driven out to the blast zone. They had to be close. Then he saw two smoking piles on the ground. The blue of the Shawnee Quarry jumpsuits, blackened around the edges, was still visible. Without pausing to think, he pulled his cell phone out of one pocket and its battery from another. As a safety measure, they were not allowed to keep the battery in their cell phones inside the quarry. It was not really a problem except on blast days, but the quarry management made it an everyday rule so the employees would develop the habit of keeping them separate. Gregg slipped the battery onto the phone and turned it on. He started shooting pictures as he approached the lumps on the ground.

As he got closer, he could see the nametags on the jumpsuits. It was them—Harry and Stephen. He was overtaken with another wave of nausea. The first round of vomiting had emptied his stomach, which did nothing to stop the dry heaves. He took more pictures after he recovered. He made sure to get the name tags.

Fear shot through him as he realized whatever had done this to Harry and Stephen might do the same to him. He turned and began to run. Raw fear, panic overtook every bit of sanity he had so desperately cultivated and clung to since the accident. He ran back to the dump truck. He tried one more time, in vain, to start it.

Standing outside the cab was Jack, the bulldozer operator. Gregg climbed out and called to him, "Harry and Stephen are dead! It looks like they just incinerated—completely. They're over by the blast zone. I got some pictures. I gotta out of here. I…I…I..." Then he simply stopped speaking and turned to look at the object again. He took a couple pictures of it and turned off his phone. He began walking toward the ramp.

His mind had kicked over into "robot mode". At least that was what Gregg called it. His psychiatrist called it a mild dissociative disorder. He would just turn off all emotion and become like a robot when he reached a point where he was no longer able to cope with what was happening around him. It had been a long time since it had happened to him. The part of Gregg that was still aware of what was occurring around him knew robot mode did not last forever. Had he been able to feel anything, he would have been glad. He would have to deal with all of what he had just seen, but he did not have to do it yet.

He walked out of the pit. There was a sheriff's car pulling into the parking area. The car's siren was on and gumball machine lights were flashing. Gregg understood it was here because of that thing in the pit. He recognized the short, round, blob of a man in the driver's seat—Horace Jones, one of the deputies. Gregg heard other sirens approaching. He knew if he were to have a chance of getting to safety, he had to leave now. He walked quickly to his car, got in and hoped it would start. It did. Whatever had happened to the engines of the vehicles in the pit had not extended this far. He spun his wheels as he drove to the back of the office building. There he found the two tracks of gravel that formed a seldom used service road. It led to an exit that was almost on the opposite side of the plant from the main gate. He pulled onto the gravel path and began to drive home.

Chapter 2

Hedwick Franklin was just dozing off in the hot bath when her phone rang. The scream from The Who's "We Won't Get Fooled Again" reverberated on the hard tile of the bathroom. That ring tone meant only one thing. It was time for the next assignment. She did not bother to get out of the tub. She could not get dry enough quickly enough to get to the phone before it went to voice mail. All the information she needed would be in the message anyway.

In a few minutes she had finished her bath, dried off and slipped on her robe. The lime green terrycloth robe was the one thing in the small apartment that was a luxury item. The apartment had come furnished. Other than food and a few toiletries, Hedwick had brought nothing extra into it except a few changes of clothes, a single case of equipment, her laptop, phone, a couple books and this robe. Everything could be put in a bag, ready to leave, in less than five minutes. The starkness of this existence wore on her. She could not, however, bring herself to put any effort into making a place feel like home when she really never knew how long she might be there. This stay at this apartment had lasted three-and-a-half months, just slightly above average.

The last assignment had been completed nine days before. Since then she had been taking a much needed rest. She had been working out the kinks and muscle soreness and generally pampering herself after a grueling three months, spent mostly in the back of a panel van. It had been the kind of assignment she hated. In the end, nothing significant happened. There had initially been the potential for something big, but the information on which they had based the operation turned out to be only partially reliable. The person providing the intelligence had slipped up. Their own agenda had been exposed, an agenda that had nothing to do with the reality of what Hedwick and her team had been brought in to investigate. The operation ended with a whimper and not a shout.

It did not mean that the operation had not had some successes. A previously unknown group of potentially dangerous individuals had been exposed. Valuable information had been gathered. Although it was not what had been anticipated, it was still a win. The newly identified organization had been teasing information out of the US archives through a backdoor. A clerk on the inside, with whom Hedwick was working, had been using his security clearance to leave small breeches, through which unredacted documents could be obtained. In this way they sought to discover the identity of the leak. Sure enough, one of the civilian employees was caught with documents on a flash drive—ones she should have had. When questioned, she caved and gave up the names of the people to whom she sold the documents. And one of those she named happened to be the informant who had given Hedwick the faulty intelligence that had started the operation in the first place. When she had found that out, she had the mother of all "it's a small world" feelings.

The group was not professional. They had pressed a slight advantage too far. Now they were under pronounced pressure to just go back to their old lives. They were not dangerous—in fact they came across to the average layperson as crazy. And that was where the real security was. While Hedwick's team could not get their hands on solid evidence against the group, any claim they made—no matter how factual it was—made them sound like the complete weirdos they were.

The truth about such fringe groups, Hedwick knew, had been used that way for years. The particularly juicy bits could be leaked, but leaked in such a way that no real hard evidence was exposed. It was usually enough, however, to get the conspiracy theorists to bite. When the information went public, it made groups like this one sound insane, especially when they were unable to counter what was being said about them. This was often more effective than trying to hide the truth.

The end of the operation had been anticlimactic. She was glad. There had been plenty of other operations that had not ended so calmly. She wondered what the next assignment would be as she reached for her phone and played the message.

"Class 1. AF Reserve base, Fort Wayne Indiana. Primary: Robert Braun. ASAP."

That was all the message there was. It was enough to tell Hedwick everything she needed to know. "Class 1" meant that there was a confirmed contact. She wondered what it would be this time. She dressed quickly. She threw all of her possessions into the two duffels kept under the bed. She took a minute, before she put the laptop in, to check directions to the Air Force base in Fort Wayne. It seemed a straight shot down the interstate. Then she slipped the laptop into its case. She took one quick final look around the apartment and walked out. She knew she would not be back.

Hedwick had packed her things almost on autopilot. Now as she drove she thought about the message. The name Robert Braun had grabbed her attention. She had not worked with Robert since the operation in Arizona, the one that almost cost her life. The one that cost her the love she had shared with Robert.

She and Robert had been a couple since the summer before they had gotten the call to go to Arizona. They had been together almost 15 months, a record for Hedwick. Her job, living in the shadows, had long made anything like a long-term relationship impossible. She knew it was dangerous to be with Robert, but they shared so much and had spent so much time together they had not been able to help herself. It had seemed so right.

The operation in Arizona had started like a number of others. There had been sightings of an unidentified object in the desert north of Phoenix. There had been other sightings on concurrent nights just outside of Tuscon and just west of the White Mountains. The descriptions had been too consistent to be random. So Robert, Hedwick and a team were sent to the area to find out what was happening.

The initial investigation had gone smoothly. Hedwick thought this would likely be one situation where of the objects had no discernible explanation. The people Hedwick worked for kept an open mind to the possibilities of extraterrestrials. At the same time, they made no effort to make contact or interfere with them.

There had been objects and sightings in the area for decades. Most had been explained. There were some, however, that had not been explained: the grey cases. As far as Hedwick knew there had not ever been any actual contact with any extraterrestrial beings. There had been observation of vessels not earthly in origin. And there was physical evidence of landings. Despite it all, there had never been any legitimate contact made with beings from these vessels. There were at least four types of objects she knew of which had been observed with varying frequency. The Arizona phenomena were most likely from the Triangle group of objects. These were by far the most common sightings. They were also the most easily explained away to the general public.

Two weeks into the operation, Robert had done the usual press conference. He had stated that there had been several tests of a new military aircraft design conducted in the area. He showed a blown up photograph that looked strikingly like a big brother to the F117 stealth fighter. He had stated it was an enhanced version of a photo that had been on the local news. For all but the truly hardcore UFO junkies, this had been sufficient explanation.

After the news conference things went suddenly sideways. She and Robert had been in the car headed back to the hotel when a crazy person popped up from the back seat of the car. Somehow, in the dark shadows of the parking garage, neither Robert nor Hedwick had noticed the figure on the floor of the back seat of the car. He held pistols, pressed against the sides of each of their necks. He was beyond agitated. Hedwick was in the driver's seat and could see the man's eyes in the rear view mirror. She had seen crazed. This man was a step past it. He was manic, which made him dangerous and, worse, unpredictable.

A normal, trained assassin or mercenary acts in a certain, expected manner. Hedwick and Robert would each have known how to handle the situation if it had been a professional in the back seat. Crazy was something else entirely. There were no rules for dealing with crazy.

"What are those things. Don't tell me they are aircraft. I saw what you did with that picture…. It was all fake." The man said.

"We can take you and show you. That's the only way we can explain what they are." Robert said. He had taken the lead in this situation. It was not what Hedwick would have done. A moving vehicle adds an extra layer of danger to an already dangerous situation.

"Drive." The man said. He pressed the barrel of the gun just a little deeper into Hedwick's neck.

She leaned just slightly forward to reach for the key that was already in the ignition. The man watched her as she did so. This was just what Robert had been waiting for. He grabbed the guns and forced them toward the seat. The man's right elbow was dislocated in the process. By reflex his left finger pulled the trigger. The bullet blasted into Hedwick's neck at an angle. Miraculously it missed all major blood vessels and her windpipe. The bullet travelled down into her left lung. It stopped just under the skin after breaking a rib. She heard a snap, muffled by the ringing in her ears from the sound of the gunshot. That was the last thing she remembered before waking up in a hospital bed. It was only later she found out the snap she had heard was the man's left arm as Robert broke it.

When she awoke, Robert sat at her bedside. It only took one look from him for her to know that they could not be together any longer. It was not, she knew, because he did not love her any more. Indeed it was the opposite. He had explained it once. Love in their line of work was deadly dangerous. It clouded judgment. She knew without a word being spoken what was going through his head. He had almost lost her. Now he would have to distance himself from her so he would not run that risk again.

Hedwick shook her head. That was all in the past. History lessons she had learned well. It would be good to see Robert again. Over the months she had thought a lot about how things had ended. She knew, however, she would not be able to talk to him about those thoughts. Still, she felt she was ready to see him again and finally to put their relationship to rest in her own mind.

She reached the freeway and revved the car to 75. She punched the CD button on the radio and turned the volume up as the first bars of "Welcome to the Jungle" began to thump from the speakers. The familiar excitement that preceded every new operation began to hum through her, seeming to beat time to the rhythm of the music.

Chapter 3

The smokestack at the Shawnee Cement factory was the tallest thing in the county, taller than the half-dozen water towers dotting the horizon, showing the location of nearby small towns. It was taller than the few sparse stands of the old growth oaks and maples, remnants of the Great Black Swamp that could still be found in the area.

This part of the Midwest was flat, scrubbed smooth by a glacier tens of thousands of years in the past. There were places where one could have more than a 180 degree view from horizon to horizon thanks to the curvature of the earth. There were some places, more than 20 miles away, from which on clear days the smokestack was visible.

Tommy Irons did not need clear weather to see the smokestack. He could see it on all but the very foggiest days. He lived much closer than 20 miles, close enough that he kept the blasting schedule for the quarry that fed the cement plant. He lived close enough that he had blackout curtains in his bedroom to block the constant pink-orange glow from the sodium arc lights that lit the nightly work of the plant's third shift.

Tommy worked a seven on-seven off second shift as a security officer at the town hospital. His schedule left him a lot of time off. During the summer, he spent part of that time drinking beer and watching the cement trucks and gravel trucks come and go from the cement factory. Tommy knew it was not much of a life. Still hurting from losing his wife and daughter in a car wreck, he accepted it for what it was. For now, he had convinced himself that he was satisfied with quiet loneliness.

It was early August. The clay in the soil had dried out and the ground had cracked. Tommy had been watching one particular crack in his yard grow for weeks. It was now over two inches wide. The farmers needed rain. The corn was rolling up and the beans were looking bad. There was no rain forecast—other than the scant possibility of a random thunderstorm, not predicted at least for one more week.

Tommy rolled into his driveway after his last evening of the current seven on stretch of work. He was looking forward to his week off. Looking in his rear view mirror as he backed into his parking spot, he noticed several camouflaged trucks pulling into the cement plant. As he got out of his car and watched, several more vehicles drove through the main gate.

Tommy had never seen trucks like that at the plant. He had never seen so many trucks at this time of night. He went inside to get his binoculars. By the time he returned to the porch, the trucks had all pulled around the far side of the main furnace building, gone from sight. He shrugged, went back inside and grabbed a six pack of beer and went to sit on the porch. He thought, "one nice thing about the dry weather is no mosquitoes." That was the last thing he thought before drifting into a day dream compounded with beer fuzzies.

The next morning, Tommy was jolted awake at 6:42 AM by the blast siren. The sound was a combination of fire siren and a loud buzz. Tommy did not remember a blast being scheduled for this morning, though he had not looked at the monthly schedule for a few days. The confusing thing to him was that the blasts were never this early. Then he noticed the siren was not the continuous wail that signaled a detonation, but the up and down siren of emergency.

Tommy dug in the Rolodex for the card that had the emergency notification number for the quarry. Anytime the emergency siren sounded there was a recording, stating the nature of the emergency and what, if any, action needed to be taken by residents living near the plant. The few times in the past it had sounded, it was always just a test or an announcement of a larger than normal or unscheduled blast. Those usually occurred in the afternoon.

Tommy dialed, and heard a strangely familiar voice. Phil Anderson, one of Tommy's high school classmates, said on the recording: "There is currently an emergency at the Shawnee Quarry and Cement facility. A large pocket of radioactive gas, commonly known as radon, has been encountered and is collecting in the quarry pit. This release of radon was unanticipated. The gas appears to be seeping from a massive, previously undiscovered reservoir. The Army Corp of Engineers, and the Nuclear Regulatory Commission have been brought in to assess and stabilize the situation. They have determined there is a significant threat. Evacuation is being ordered for a 3 mile radius around the Shawnee Quarry, with further evacuations to the immediate downwind areas as directed by Army personnel. Evacuees are being asked to go to the County Consolidated High School, where an evacuation center is currently being established. If you are within the evacuation area, please proceed immediately to the County Consolidated High school. Further information will be communicated to you there, as it becomes available." Tommy heard the click as the automatic recording cut off.

Tommy had known Phil most of his life. He had heard something not quite right in his voice. Perhaps it was fear due to the situation. Tommy let that thought fade as he let the implication of the message sink in.

"Well that explains the trucks last night," Tommy thought. He grabbed a large duffel bag from the hall closet, and went first to the bedroom to grab a couple changes of clothes, then to the kitchen to throw in a couple bottles of bourbon and a few Army surplus MRE's (Meals Ready to Eat; high calorie, low flavor, keep a soldier alive rations) to keep with him, just in case. Finally he grabbed the two boxes of spare ammunition for the .38 he kept in the glove box of his truck.

He left the doors of the house unlocked. He figured that if there were going to be looters taking advantage of the situation, he might be spared having to replace a window if they could just walk in. Besides, there was not anything in the house worth much and he had insurance for all of it anyway. The only things that could be destroyed that Tommy valued were the pictures he had. He had copies on DVD's in a safe deposit box, so even they were not in real danger. The only other things were a small lock of his daughter's hair he carried encased in a piece of clear acrylic the size and shape of a half dollar, and his wife's engagement ring that he kept on a chain around his neck with his dog tags.

To Tommy, the rest of it was just stuff: replaceable. Before his wife and daughter died, Tommy was caught up in the more is better American Dream delusion. He had been trying to get a bigger house and had been looking at a big, flat screen TV. He drove a new pickup. He had taken his wife and daughter on several expensive vacations. He had acquired the debt to prove he had been living the delusion.

He knew better now that he was alone. There had been enough insurance money and a small settlement with the other driver, and Tommy had paid off his debts. He no longer had the desire for the big house. He wanted to stay in the home he had shared with his family. What little television he watched (mostly baseball in the summer and football in the fall) he watched on an old 19" TV. He had traded in the new, overpowered pickup for an older secondhand farmer's pickup. He lived debt free now, but had paid the most terrible price for it.

Chapter 4

Michelle Perry sat at her desk. She stared at the blank Open Office document on her screen. She had been staring at it for ten minutes. Despite the appearance of inactivity, her mind worked furiously.

She was trying to come up with the perfect lead sentence for the story she needed to write for this afternoon's deadline. She glanced at her watch. It was only 9:45 AM. She had just over six hours to write a 750 word piece on the controversy over the new school building project.

She had read essentially the same article she was going to write in several of the small town papers from around the state. The controversy arose not in the reality that the state was funding the building of new school buildings. Many of the small towns across the state had outdated school buildings. The problem was that there was no money being provided for hiring or retaining teachers. There was no money for the ongoing operating expenses for the new buildings.

Michelle had read several analogies describing the situation and was trying to decide which she would quote for the article. She was leaning toward a statement made by one of the teachers at a school board meeting: "It is like giving a homeless person a Corvette, without any gas in the tank, and no money to pay for the insurance." Of course there were holes in all of the analogies she had heard. But, for Michelle, this one had the best punch.

Personally, Michelle was on the side of those who believed the building fund should be split, or partially set aside to help pay for teachers and facility operations. The other side of the argument was that those expenses should not change from the expenditures at the previous building. The school levies that had previously been funding the old school building's operations should be sufficient to fund the current operations. Of course, the counter argument was that there were circumstances not taken into account by the state in their reasoning.

These differing views were numerous and sometimes subtle. Michelle realized 750 words would be insufficient to explore the issue fully. She decided the best treatment she could give the matter would be to write a simple summary of the recent school board meeting in which the matter was discussed. She would spice it up with a few tasty quotes from both the school board, and audience members. She knew that Sam Keep, her editor, would be writing an op-ed piece on the same subject, and would cover most of the arguments and subtler points. She trusted he would do a good job. The job left to her, as usual, was to just write the facts.

Michelle sighed and began to type. She always went through the same mental gymnastics before she began to write. Most of the time, simply thinking about a story for a sufficient time allowed the irrelevant details to sift out from the main points. She had once described it as: when she started to think about writing a news story, she had a whole lot of facts, not all of which were relevant to what really needed to be written. All of the facts went into a sifter. Some of the facts were unimportant and were like sand. Some facts were important and were like pebbles. For Michelle, the process of thinking through things shook her mental sifter so the sand fell out and left only the pebbles. She would then mentally sort and arrange the pebbles and the outline for her story would present itself.

This process analogy was somewhat the reverse of the one she had learned in her creative writing classes in college. There the analogy was that, when one started a story, they had an empty jar which represented the story. The first thing into the jar was the big rocks like main characters, plot and theme. Next, smaller pebbles were added. These were things like minor characters, setting, and subplots. Finally the rest of the jar was filled with sand. The sand was the details, the little things that made a basic story something truly enjoyable.

Michelle had been typing for only a couple minutes when her phone rang. She picked it up. She was upset at herself for not silencing it before she began writing.

"Hello. This is Michelle," She said. She could tell from the display that the call was coming from in house, so she did not resort to her usual, chipper, professional greeting.

"There is something going on over at Shawnee. The police have been out there since yesterday morning, and there are some Army Corp of Engineers people out there now. The emergency siren went off and the message, when you call the emergency number, says there is radon in the pit. You are on it." The line went dead.

Her boss, Sam, did not sound any more or less excited than he normally did, but Michelle knew he felt this was a big deal. He almost never sent her on a new assignment when he was already expecting copy from her. He had not even mentioned her current deadline.

"First thing is first," she thought. She pulled up her phone list on her computer, and dialed the emergency number for the quarry. She listened to the message and made a few notes. Then she began the research process. By the time this was over, she would be an expert on all things cement.

Chapter 5

Tommy went in once he got to the school. He was told that there were some cots in the gym and there would be food in the cafeteria in about an hour. He wandered into the gym and picked out a cot toward the far end, away from the locker rooms. He wanted to be as far away from them as possible so sounds coming from them would not disturb his sleep. Anyway, he was not planning on spending more than the first night here anyway.

He had already decided that, after he got a little more information, he would go to stay at his uncle's place that was several miles north of the evacuation zone. It was just a little hunting cabin by the river and it was unused at the moment. It would stay empty until hunting season. Tommy had use of it whenever he wanted. He would sometimes go out to just listen to the birds for hours—the windows open while he laid on the couch—and daydream about the stolen weekends he had spent there with his wife right after they had been married and couldn't afford to go away for the weekend.

Tommy was lost in thought, remembering those weekends with Cindy alone in the cabin. He sat down on the cot. He was snapped out of his reverie by Gregg Childress plopping his large frame down next to him. Gregg had been another schoolmate of Tommy's. Gregg also worked at the cement plant. Tommy immediately noticed the terrified look in his eyes.

"Hey, Gregg. What's up?" Tommy asked.

Gregg, wide eyes searching, looked from side to side as if expecting the boogeyman. Tommy had seen Gregg with a look similar to this. He had seen the twitching, wide eyes at the hospital, a couple years before, when he had been working. Gregg had not been taking his drugs for schizophrenia and had ended up getting into a fight. He had gotten beaten badly. The police brought him into the hospital to be patched up. The look in Gregg's eyes then was of rage and insensibility and fear. Now, the look was almost entirely fear. Tommy was not scared of Gregg, but was concerned that maybe he had gone off his medications again.

"It isn't radon, Tommy." Gregg hissed in a harsh whisper. He got up and went for the exit, looking over his shoulder several times as he walked.

Tommy was stunned. He watched Gregg leave, wondering what he was meant. Tommy looked at the cot where Gregg had sat, realizing Gregg had left his cell phone. Had he left it on purpose? It was on—in camera mode—and the picture that was showing scared him. Tommy scrolled through the rest of the pictures and became progressively more frightened.

The first picture was blurry, hastily taken, or perhaps taken with shaking hands. Still, Tommy could clearly see a large metal looking object that was unlike anything he had ever seen. At the end of a conical pillar was a fan shaped blade that glowed with a cool, pale blue light. It reminded Tommy of the foxfire he had seen in the Smoky Mountains as a kid. The conical pillar was attached at the other end to what looked like one of the points of a crescent moon, just slightly back from the point. About a third of the crescent was sticking out of the limestone. The rest of whatever it was appeared to be embedded in the rock.

Tommy thought of Stephen King's Tommyknockers and wondered what to do next. The last picture Tommy came to was the most distressing. It was a close up of the area where the object met the limestone. There were two bodies of plant workers. They were dead. They had to be. Their skin was blackened. Smoke rose from them in the picture. The worst part was that their clothes looked as if they had only been charred at the edges by whatever had fried the workers' bodies.

Tommy's stomach churned. He had seen horrible things during his days in the Army, and in the emergency room at the hospital, but this was different. This wasn't just close to home, but horribly strange and new and incomprehensible. For all he knew, those bodies could be guys he knew, drank beer and played pool with at Lucky's Bar. He felt a sense of panic start to well up inside him. He knew he had to get out of the high school gym, or at least find out if anyone had noticed Gregg talking to him. He needed a few minutes to figure out what to do next. The biggest question was whether anyone knew that Gregg had taken those pictures, and if they did, whether they knew Tommy now had them.

He bent over and slipped the phone into an open pocket on his duffel bag. He looked around, trying not to reveal the same scared look that had been in Gregg's eyes. He set his duffel up on the cot beside him and rooted around for his toiletry bag. And discretely moved the phone into it.

He got up with the toiletry bag and walked to the locker room. He ducked into one of the stalls to see if he would be followed. After a full five minutes by his watch, no one else had come into the locker room.

As he sat and waited, he began to wonder if the photos were real. He looked at them again. They were far too detailed for Gregg to have faked them. Just as Gregg would not have been able to fake the failed brakes on his car, when he hit Tommy's wife and daughter. Tommy, after a brief painful moment, blocked those thoughts from his mind. It had been an accident and, he told himself for what seemed the millionth time, he had forgiven Gregg.

Tommy tried to figure out his next move. He put the phone back into his toiletry bag, and walked out of the locker room. He sat down on his cot, stuffed the bag into the duffel and lay down to try to take a nap. He had slept poorly the night before. He was exhausted despite the shock of the pictures—or perhaps because of it. He knew he needed to rest before he could make a good decision, even though he had a good idea of the direction that decision would take.

Chapter 6

Gregg walked down the long corridor from the gymnasium to the back parking lot of the High School. At the end of the hall was a floor to ceiling mural of the school logo: a giant maroon water moccasin coiled around a black capital G. The snake appeared to be staring right at Gregg. The long body appeared to be moving ever so slightly, as if preparing to strike. Gregg had once worn that logo proudly on the back of his letter jacket. Now it was a bit of horror for him. He knew the movement was not real. He knew his own mind was generating it.

He was so tired. After he had left the quarry, he drove around for hours trying to clear his mind. He tried to figure out what he had seen and what he needed to do next. He had stopped by the river and looked at the pictures on his phone. He was appalled. He almost threw the phone into the river.

"That is what they want. They want you to get rid of it. They want to be able to hide what is going on there," a whisper had come to Gregg's ear. Gregg was surprised. This was a different voice than the ones he had heard before. Usually the voices were deep and resonant. This voice was high pitched, clear, more like a bell than a kettle drum.

Gregg had been able to suppress the ideas that there were people who were always watching him for a long time. Now the idea came back full force.

"Put the phone back in your pocket. You have to keep those pictures safe. If you destroy them, then you have no evidence. Evidence is protection."

He had struggled to put the phone back in his pocket. He had wanted desperately to be rid of the thing.

"I don't want it. I want to get rid of it. I want to forget."

"So give it to someone you trust."

"Who?" Gregg had asked.

The voice had no answer. There had been only the sound of the breeze, rustling the prematurely dry cornstalks in the field across the road.

He went home and drank, even knowing he should not. The labels on at least two of his medications told him not to combine them with alcohol. Instead he listened to his gut and drank. Eventually he drank enough to make it difficult to stand. He had staggered out to the pool and climbed in.

He had spent most of the night in the pool. It had been warm when he had gotten in. He had tried again to clear his mind of what he had seen. He tried to think of to whom he should give the phone. He had asked a few more times for the voice to tell him and had gotten no answer. The stars kept making patterns that looked alternately like the dead bodies of his coworkers and the giant object in the pit, the thing that had killed them. As he grew more tired and the alcohol took a tighter grip on him, the images became more vivid, more realistic. Without realizing it was coming over him, Gregg fell asleep.

When he awoke, he was shivering. The water had cooled. Gregg climbed out, stiff and chilled. He went into his trailer knowing what he would do. He would go to the school. The radio had said it is where the evacuees would be. He would find someone he trusted and give them the phone. That way he would be free. Then he could just forget about it.

At last he had accomplished his task—getting rid of the phone. Tommy was the perfect person to pass it on to. Gregg knew Tommy would know what to do. Tommy always knew what to do. Gregg trusted him. Now Gregg would go home and sleep. Despite the weather, he still felt cold. He looked again at the snake and paused. The snake seemed to be writhing more. He thought he heard a voice.

"Why did you do that?" the voice asked.

"I don't know what you're talking about," Gregg said. He had thought the voice had come from the snake but he could not be sure. It was raspy, hissing, almost like air being let out of a tire.

"Why did you give Tommy the phone? That was your responsibility." The voice said. Gregg was now sure it was the snake.

"I had to get rid of it. They would come and get me if I didn't get rid of it." Gregg said. He was trying to remain calm, but felt the beginnings of panic start to creep up from the pit of his stomach.

"So now they will come and get Tommy. Is that what you want? Do you want them to get Tommy? He has been so good to you. He forgave you for what you did to him. He doesn't deserve that."

"But, he is stronger than I am. He was in the Army. He will know what to do. He, He, He… is able to do things I can't do. I had to get rid of it." Gregg protested. The panic was stirring deeply now. It was rising. He looked at the snake again. It was writhing in time to the churning in Gregg's intestines.

"What are you going to do now? You can't forget what you saw. Tommy will tell them that you gave him those pictures. He will tell them that you were the one who took them. He will tell them—"

Gregg did not wait to hear the end of it. He bolted out the door. Three steps outside, he tripped over a curb and fell, scraping his knees and his palms. He got up, still hearing a hissing voice behind him. He ran to his car and drove away as fast as he could.

By the time he reached his home he was calmer, helped by a double dose of his anxiety medication. Every time he thought about the pictures, he got caught in circular logic. He had to get rid of the pictures. He was sure of that. He also was sure that he should not get rid of the pictures. He had given the picture to Tommy, but that was where he got caught in his thought process. He was not sure about that point. He was not sure that Tommy would stay safe. But he came right back to the awareness that he had needed to get rid of the pictures.

As he struggled with it, he realized being rid of the pictures did not ensure that he was safe. Even if Tommy did not tell them where he had gotten the pictures, it was very likely that they would be able to figure it out from Gregg's phone. They would still come. He had a sudden certainty that it was all over. He knew they would come for him. That meant he only had one choice left.

Chapter 7

The public address system woke Tommy after only forty-five minutes of sleep. "Food is now available in the cafeteria, please feel free to help yourself."

Still, he had slept very soundly and felt refreshed. As soon as he was fully awake, he knew what he had to do. He had to wait. He had to wait to see how the Army was going to handle the situation. His course of action would largely be determined by their course of action. For the time being, he would behave just like the rest of the evacuees.

He went to the cafeteria and got a stale bagel, a cup of coffee and an apple. He sat at one of the bench tables and ate. He considered his alternatives based on how the thing in the quarry was handled by the government. If they revealed the truth, he would simply say nothing—the information would be out there with no cover-up. If the government decided to cover it up, Tommy also knew what he had to do.

After eating and getting a second cup of too weak coffee, Tommy went back to the gym. Someone had set up some folding chairs, clustered in groups of five or six. Tommy took one from the bunch closest to his cot, sat and put his feet up. He waited.

Several hours passed. He chatted with some of his neighbors. He read the coverage of the evacuation in the afternoon newspaper. He napped again. He ate supper in the cafeteria. The evening dwindled. He had hoped he would be out of the school and on his way to his uncle's cabin by now, but there was no news. He had become used to this kind of waiting during his days in the Army, where he had learned how to simply be. He played cards with a few guys from the bar, then lay down on the cot to sleep.

Thirty minutes later, he still hadn't fallen asleep. He got up and walked around the gym. He washed down a couple antihistamines with a big swig of bourbon and lay back down. He was not used to napping during the day. This inability to fall asleep was the consequence.

Once he finally drifted off, he slept well, except for a dream in which he was in the quarry. He saw the two plant workers get baked by whatever that thing was. The dream replayed a couple times in variations, including one in which he was one of the workers. That was the worst of the dreams. He felt as if he drank a quart of hot sauce mixed with gasoline then swallowed a match. It was as if he was boiling from the inside out.

Despite the bad dreams, Tommy woke refreshed. He was just coming back from a breakfast of rubber eggs and greasy, undercooked bacon, when he heard the announcement over the P. A.: "Colonel Jackson, commander of the Army unit currently in charge of the situation at the Shawnee Quarry, will be holding a news conference in the auditorium in five minutes. Anyone interested please go to the auditorium at this time. Thank you."

Tommy went to his cot, grabbed Gregg's phone and slipped it into his pocket. He went to the auditorium. The media had been kept out of the areas where the evacuees were staying, but in the auditorium they were everywhere. Cameras flashed. Tommy recognized reporters from the local television channels as well as a couple from the networks. There were TV cameras with every news agency logo he could imagine.

Tommy pressed himself against the wall out of the line of sight of most of the cameras. Again he waited, but not for long. A large, fortyish man dripping Army, walked to the podium on the stage. He sipped water from the glass on the podium, cleared his throat and began.

"Ladies and gentlemen, thank you for coming today. For those of you who have been evacuated from your homes, thank you for your patience. As you are all aware, late in the afternoon two days ago, a large pocket of radon gas was encountered during the quarrying operations at the Shawnee Quarry…."

That was all Tommy needed to hear. They were going to cover up what was really going on in the pit, what was in the pictures. They had his phone number. He had told a couple of the guys last night his plans to go to the cabin. They could find him when they decided what they would do about his house. If they let him move back in—or if they paid him off—they could find him. He slipped out the side door of the auditorium and dropped Gregg's phone in the trash can as he left the school.

Chapter 8

Following the sounding of the Emergency Siren at Shawnee Quarry, Michelle Perry had been awake for twenty-eight hours. She had stayed awake at first by drinking triple shot red eyes. At four in the morning, she had popped a Ritalin she had liberated from her nephew's supply. It was not going to be missed—a leftover from the old prescription after the doctor changed his dose. She did not use them often. And never more than one. But for the really big stories, just sometimes, she could justify it. This was a big story.

Michelle watched Tommy as he came into the auditorium. She met him a few years earlier when she was doing a series of stories on the "hidden heroes of Greenburg". Originally, she had planned on another in a series of fluff pieces on semi-important jobs in the community. Once Michelle started talking to Tommy, she knew there was much more going on under the surface. She had invited him out for drinks to do the interview.

Toward the end of the interview Michelle asked the usual question, "Tell me about your family." By this time Tommy had downed three boilermakers.

He had told Michelle all about his wife Cindy: how they had met at a summer camp, how he had chased her, romanced her and finally convinced her to marry him. He told her about when he found out he was going to be a father. He had nearly thrown up from the combination of excitement and fear. About how, when his daughter Samantha was born, he finally understood what it meant to be complete; to feel immortal and still be aware of his mortality.

Then Tommy told Michelle about the accident. By that time, he was near the bottom of his fourth boilermaker. He told her his daughter had died right away and he always had counted that, in some small way, as a blessing. His wife lived through the crash. She made it to the hospital. She had asked for Tommy, then died just before he got there. That was the worst part, he told Michelle, the not being able to say goodbye.

Tommy was drunk, and had told Michelle more than he intended. The one thing he wished he had not told her was how he would rehearse, over and over, telling his wife goodbye, that it was okay to go. Just like in the movies. Michelle had gone home with Tommy that night. Tommy drank more, and they talked. Michelle knew she could never write the story. Tommy's speech got slower. His responses to Michelle's questions came slower and slower until he stopped talking in mid-sentence and fell asleep.

Michelle let herself out, leaving her card in front of the coffee pot. She was surprised when Tommy called the next day.

"Hello, Michelle? Sorry about last night." Tommy said.

"There is nothing to be sorry about, Tommy."

"I told you a lot more than I meant to. I told you more than I've told anyone since it happened. I know I agreed to the interview, but please don't write anything about the accident. I'll do the interview again about my job, but please leave my wife and daughter out of it."

It surprised Michelle. She had not intended to write about what Tommy had told her. She remembered how awful she had felt about the biased coverage that had haunted one of her friends, one who had been in an accident after having one drink. She had been crushed by the innuendo of drunk driving. It had not mattered to the gossips that she had passed a breathalyzer on the scene.

"Don't worry Tommy." Michelle answered. "That's all off the record as far as I am concerned. I'll take you up on the offer for the mulligan on the interview. If I have your schedule right, you should be off Saturday. Can we get together then?"

"Sure. Seven o'clock at Lucky's?" Tommy said.

"Ok, I'll see you then."

Michelle saw Tommy leave the auditorium and watched him drop something shiny into the garbage can as he passed it. She was intrigued instantly, both by why he had left early and what he had dropped into the trash.

"… We will be relocating all of the households within a three mile radius of Shawnee. In addition, radon monitors and regular testing will be made available to any individual living within a radius of…"

Michelle's attention was drawn back to the present by the colonel's statement. There were going to relocate everyone? Her research showed about 200 families in that area. This was going to be expensive.

"…In addition, Shawnee's parent company has assured me that any employee who loses their current position due to the closing of this facility will be offered a retirement package, or full relocation packages to one of their other facilities…." The colonel droned on.

Michelle was having trouble focusing on what she was hearing. Her mind kept wandering to Tommy and what he had dropped into the trash. Part of it was being tired and part was the Ritalin. She knew the way these things went. No real news was being offered and the conference might go on for quite a while.

She double checked that her recorder was working, sat it on a small ledge beside the exit door and went to the can where Tommy had dropped the mystery object. She saw only one thing that looked out of place among the rest of the garbage.

Suddenly the sound from the auditorium tripled in volume. The colonel must be done with his speech and opening up to questions. She grabbed the cell phone from the trash can and went back to the auditorium.

Chapter 9

Tommy sat in his truck, the engine running. He was struggling with what he had done. Should he have thrown away the cell phone? The biggest question that kept coming to mind was, "What is that thing?" He began to regret what he had done. He was sure he didn't want to take the pictures to the police or the news, but he kept wondering what would happen if someone else found the phone. He should have deleted the pictures.

He sat for another moment, trying to clear his mind. Dennis DeYoung sang to him from the radio. "...And we'll tryyyyy.... best that we caaaaannnn..... to caaaaaaarrrrrrryyy onnnn...."

Tommy's mind was drawn to those first few days after he had buried his wife and daughter. It was all he had been capable of: carrying on, just living moment to moment. Then he got to where he could live hour by hour, and finally to the point he could live day to day—the way he lived now.

"...I thought that they were angels.... but to my surprise..... we climbed aboard their starship, and headed for the skiiiiiiiiiiiiiiiiies..."

He got out of the truck, and headed back to the school. He needed to recover the phone. He needed to think a little more about what to do and he would not be able to focus unless he had that phone.

Ten feet from the double glass doors of the school, he stopped dead still. Michelle was digging in the garbage can where Tommy had dropped the phone.

He was frozen. "Now what?" he asked himself silently.

He watched as she looked back toward the auditorium, hoping she would leave. His heart sank as he watched her grab something from the garbage and put it in her pocket before she walked away.

Tommy felt sick. He bolted for the garbage can. The phone was gone. She had it. She had not, he thought, looked at the pictures. This complicated things. He had to try to get her to give the phone back to him before she saw those images.

Tommy and Michelle had gone out several times on and off over the last few years. She had been the one woman who seemed to "get him". For an excuse to talk to her today he would offer to help her with the story. That is why she was here, the story. His mind was a jumble, but a plan had formed.

Tommy became aware of the roar coming from the auditorium. He went in and started looking for Michelle. She was only a few feet away. He did not think she had seen him return to the auditorium. He looked for a way to get closer to her.

"... as I said earlier, those in the affected area will have their homes purchased, at a fair market value, and be given the opportunity, under supervision, to go to their houses, for limited periods, to pack up their belongings and make ready to move..."

Tommy stopped watching Michelle for a moment and focused on the colonel. This was something he had not expected.

"... will be allowed into the area in small groups, under escort, based on location. The groups will be..."

A new plan came to him suddenly, a plan to get into the quarry and see the thing for himself. And he knew he would need Michelle's help.

Chapter 10

The first step of Tommy's plan was to get Michelle alone, show her what was on the phone and convince her to help him. He would wait 'til the press conference was over. He could use the time. He needed to think, to flesh out the details of how he could get in to the quarry, find out what the thing was—and how to get back out. He would not think about anything beyond that. He could not, because the future would be determined by what he learned.

The colonel droned on, answering questions without giving any real answers. Tommy thought this man had taken a full course from the best spin doctors on the planet. Just as things seemed likely to go on forever, the colonel ended it.

"The resident call center will be open to schedule times for those affected to go to their homes and also schedule settlement appointments. Those phone numbers have already been made available to the press. No more questions. Thank you."

Tommy was surprised by the suddenness of it, but also pleased it was over. He moved to the door to catch Michelle as she left. He watched as she paused to talk to another reporter. Then as she reached the door, Tommy grabbed her elbow and pulled her aside.

"You have to come with me. Just trust me," he said.

"What?" She asked.

"I have to talk to you. It is about the phone."

"What?" Michelle asked again.

Tommy leaned close to her ear. "It isn't radon in the quarry, and the proof is in that phone. You have to come with me."

He guided her through the door of the auditorium and pulled her to the side, down the hallway toward the cafeteria.

"There are pictures on that phone. They're of something in that pit. We need to talk, but not here. Please come with me."

"I have a story to finish." Michele said.

"This is bigger than your story."

"What? A major employer is shut down, and two or three

hundred families have to be relocated. It's bigger than that?" Michelle asked. She looked at Tommy. There was something in his face that made her afraid, and made her know he was telling her the truth. She stared at him.

"Okay." She said at length. She reached into her bag and pulled out the phone. "What's on here?"

"Put it away, not here!" Tommy hissed through clenched teeth.

Michelle quickly put the phone back.

"My truck is outside. We need to get away from here first."

"OK."

Tommy, still holding Michelle's elbow, walked her out to the truck. He put the befuddled Michelle into the passenger seat and got in. He sighed deeply, then started the truck. He suddenly felt very tired.

Tommy started driving, not really headed toward anywhere particular. He explained to Michelle how he had gotten the phone.

"So why did you throw it away? And how did you know I had it?" Michelle asked.

"I panicked I guess. Probably not thinking straight. I thought it was the right thing to do, but almost immediately started to second guess myself. I was headed back to get the phone when I saw you get it…. Look at the pictures." Tommy said. He pulled off the road onto a farmer's lane between two fields, and stopped the truck.

Michelle opened the phone, and flipped through the pictures. She had to get out of the truck. She retched, regretting the garlic bread and pizza she had eaten at four that morning.

"What…is… that?" She asked once she was able to regain her equilibrium.

"I don't know. But, I have to find out. Will you help me? Something is being covered up and I know I have to figure out what it is." Tommy answered.

Michelle was silent for several minutes, during which she flipped through the pictures twice more. "Okay," she finally answered very quietly. "I'll help you. What do we do?"

"I think the first thing is to go talk to Gregg and find out exactly where he took those pictures. Then we can figure out how to get into the pit and where we need to go.

"Alright." Michelle answered.

Tommy looked at Michelle. He thought she looked scared and

exhausted. It was something that Tommy had seen in the mirror too many times, the point he got to himself when he was under stress, under rested or both. Especially when there was no chance for rest in the foreseeable future.

"Are you okay?" Tommy asked.

"I will be, I think…. I'm just so tired."

"Gregg lives way out by Chester. It'll be about half an hour to get there. Try and take a nap, if you can."

"I don't know if I can. I'll try."

Michelle climbed back into the truck and leaned back against the seat. Tommy began heading to the far corner of the county to Gregg's house. The exhaustion was too much for Michelle. She was sleeping within five minutes. Tommy drove slower than he could have, so that Michelle could rest. He would need her—and need her fresh—or at least not so tired as to be dangerous.

Chapter 11

Tommy pulled into the driveway that led to Gregg's trailer. He thought the setting would be a lovely place for a house, situated in the edge of a woods, overlooking the river. In the distance, on the river bottom were some wild turkeys, and there had been occasional sightings of bald eagles fishing in the river.

Tommy touched Michelle on the shoulder. She started awake with a moan.

"Are we there?" she asked.

"Yes."

They gazed at each other for a moment before they got out and walked to the door. Tommy could hear Sports Center on the TV. He knocked. There was no response. He knocked again. Nothing. Gregg's car was in the driveway. He had to be there.

Tommy looked through the window next to the door. He could see Gregg's silhouette sitting in a chair. The left side of his head was oddly misshapen. Tommy's heart sank. He tried the doorknob. It was unlocked.

He moved into the room slowly. The first thing he noticed was the overwhelming amount of blood splattered to Gregg's left, pooled on the carpet next to him.

Michelle screamed as she looked past Tommy. Tommy had a combat flashback from his Army days. Then for some reason, he remembered playing baseball in high school, with Gregg on the mound. He pictured Gregg's odd delivery, so effective, as the only left-handed pitcher on the team. In an instant, Tommy knew what they were seeing in the living room was not right.

"We have to get out of here." Tommy said.

"But we have to call the police. Look at this." Michelle said, pointing to Gregg's laptop. The message on the screen read: I've seen too much. I can't get it out of my head. I have to make it stop.

Tommy looked at Gregg's right hand. The gun there confirmed what he suspected. This was not suicide.

"We have to go." Tommy said. He grabbed Michelle's arm and pulled her out of the trailer, wiping the doorknob with his handkerchief as he left.

When they were in the truck, he said. "Gregg was murdered. I don't know by who, but I bet it is because of those pictures."

"How…what … how do you know that?" Michelle asked.

"The gun was in his right hand. He was left-handed."

Tommy was silent for minutes as he started the truck, and began driving.

"So what now?" Michelle asked.

"We have a choice to make. Do we still try and find out what that thing is, knowing it could get us killed? Or, do we try and go public with what we know, then hide? Or do we strike a deal with the Army, and see if we can trade the pictures for our lives?"

"We don't have enough evidence to go public. If the military, or whoever it is in charge of this thing, finds out what we know, we are as good as dead. I think the only chance we have is to get more evidence. Do you have a plan?"

"Not yet. I did. But it depended on knowing exactly where that thing is in the pit. What I was thinking of won't work if we go in blind. I need to think."

Chapter 12

Robert Braun closed the door to the little office he had appropriated in the main complex of the cement factory. He poured a double whisky from the decanter his aide had found in the desk drawer of the plant manager's office. He took a small sip. It was good. Not outstanding like the eighteen-year-old single malt scotch he usually drank, but still drinkable.

He sighed deeply as he sank into the plush leather chair that was a stark contrast to the desk behind which it sat. The desk was one of those 1960's, dusty green, metal monsters with a faded Formica top. It reminded him of the elementary school teachers he had known.

He was tired. Public spectacles, like the press conference he had just endured, always exhausted him. He much preferred to work in the shadows, behind the scenes, but this…thing put him in a position where he did not trust anyone, other than himself, to talk to the press.

He unbuttoned the Army tunic with "Jackson" on the pocket and the colonel's bird emblem on the lapel. He had never been in the Army, but was not afraid of anyone checking up on him. He had alias profiles available with all the branches of the military, the NSA, ICE and most of the other agencies in Washington. The people he worked for made sure of that. Braun's job was much easier when he could be a chameleon or, better yet, invisible.

He thought the press conference had gone well. Preparations were underway to make a final sweep of the area around the quarry so that the real work could begin.

Braun took another sip of whisky, and leaned back in the chair. He closed his eyes and ran through the entire timeline of events so far. From the first call to 9-1-1 until now was only about thirty-six hours. He had been the closest operative to this pit in the middle of nowhere, this flat farmland that smelled of manure and tilled earth and the gas and diesel of tractors and old pickup trucks. For that reason alone, it fell to him to take the point.

The thing in the pit was not completely without precedent. From the very beginning there had been images of unexplained objects in some of the photos sent back by the deep space and Mars probes. The majority of activity had been observed in the images of Encladus, Titan and Europa, and those of the poles of Mars. Then there had been a single image from the lunar stationary probe that monitored the dark side of the moon. And there was the probe that had been put in orbit around the sun in the asteroid belt that gave very clear images, including one eerily similar to the part of the object sticking out of the rock—before the probe stopped transmitting.

These objects had been directly observed for at least twenty-five years, and there was indirect evidence from much further back. The thing that Braun was not able to understand was why this thing ended up as it did; almost totally buried in limestone. From the photographic evidence, Braun knew the majority of the object was buried. Why? …. That question would have to wait.

There was a knock at the office door. Hedwick Franklin stood outside, waiting for him to look up. Braun gazed at her. This was the first assignment with her since the case in Arizona. Her hair was darker and shorter than it had been then. She looked trimmer in the Army uniform than in the hippie, crystal-lover outfit she had donned during the investigation of the sightings. It suited her, showing off her muscular legs under the modest skirt, while the jacket collar hid the bullet scar on her neck.

"The target has been neutralized." Hedwick said. "However, there is a problem. There is a cell phone registered to him that was not located. We believe he may have taken some pictures of the object. Cashman is hacking the phone now, we should know more soon."

She did not want to tell him that the target had already been dead when they had gone to find him. It did not matter. She knew Robert would not care about the nature of the neutralization, as long as there was not a liability.

"Good. Are there any other loose ends?" Braun asked.

"Nothing that can not be handled." She said.

She looked closely at Braun. "He looks a lot older," she thought. "Too many years of this I suppose." She knew the toll this work had taken on her, and she knew he had been doing this much longer than she had.

"Very good. Check to be sure that the evacuation is going well, then get some sleep. You are going to need it. If you need anything, I'll be here. I may take a nap, but I'll be here." Braun said.

"OK, I'll be back in three hours with a status report." She answered.

"Fine."

Hedwick left the office. Braun listened to her heels click down the hallway. He had loved her once. He had recruited her when she was a cadet at Quantico. He had fallen for her because of the combination of naiveté and the incredible skills she possessed. She had become one of the best. Until Arizona, she had seemed to love him in return. But their affection went the only way it could have that would leave them both alive. She knew that of course. Still, she had not been able to see him the same way after that.

Braun pushed those thoughts from his mind. He took another swallow of whiskey, then got up and went to the low Naugahyde sofa sitting beneath the office windows. He lay down and began to drift off. Soon he slept deeply.

Chapter 13

Tommy knew they both needed to rest. He could tell Michelle had been up far too long, and the short nap she had taken had not been nearly enough. Tommy had the basics of his plan, but he knew he could think more clearly after he got some more rest. The nightmares of the previous night had caught up with him. He needed to give his mind a break to process what he had seen at Gregg's trailer.

He no longer felt sure about going to the cabin. He decided instead to go to the barn on his grandparents' farm. He could put the truck inside the barn, and no one would know they were there. They could sleep in the little bunk room in the back corner of the barn. It was a leftover from the days when his grandfather hired summer help for the farm.

Tommy remembered spending long, hot, summer nights here as a teenager. He worked for his grandfather along with his cousin Keith. After supper and a shower in the farm house, they would fall asleep listening to the Cleveland Indians' games on the radio. On Saturday nights they would go on double dates with the Allen twins, or the Smith sisters. Keith was a year older and had an old Corvair convertible. They would take the girls to the VanDyne drive-in theatre, put the top down, light citronella candles and watch the movie. Afterward they took the girls home, went back to the bunk room and told lies to each other about what they had done with their dates. They never stayed out too late, because they knew they had to get up for church on Sunday morning. That was the one rule. There was no curfew for Saturday night, but their grandparents made sure they got up for church on Sunday.

Tommy drove to the farm and around to the back of the barn. He got out and pushed open the big sliding door of the barn. The smell of hay and dust filled his nostrils and the rush of memories from those long ago summers hit him. For just a second he was sixteen again. He shook his head to clear away the memories. He pulled the truck in, turned it off and closed the barn door.

He and Michelle should be safe here. This barn had not been used since his grandfather had passed away. The land was all farmed now by the Caples, who had their own barns nearby. No one would bother them.

Tommy showed Michelle to the bunk room.

"It isn't much, but it is safe." Tommy said.

"I'm so tired. But I don't know if I can sleep." Michelle answered.

"Just a minute… I can help that." Tommy said.

He went to the truck. He opened the duffel bag and dug out the bottle of diphenhydramine. Then he saw the phone on the seat of the truck. An awful realization came to him—he had to get rid of the phone. He picked it up and made sure it was off. Could he afford to turn it on long enough to be sure the pictures were on the memory card, he wondered. He decided against it.

He took the diphenhydramine and a bottle of water to Michelle. He was trying to think of how to get rid of the phone, but keep the pictures.

"Here, this will help you sleep." Tommy said. He handed her two capsules and the water.

"What is it?" She asked.

"Just Benadryl, but it will help you sleep. I have to go get rid of the phone. I will drive away from here, turn it on, be sure the pictures are on the memory card, then ditch the phone and keep the memory card."

"Are you sure you have to do that?" Michelle showed a sudden realization of what could happen if they got caught with that phone. "I guess you do…." She answered her own question. "OK, I'll wait here. Be careful."

Tommy left the barn and drove west. He already knew where he would ditch the phone. He headed toward the giant dairy farms in the outskirts of the county. Who ever killed Gregg would find the phone, but they would pay to do it.

He pulled into the defunct Adams farm. At one time there had been 700 dairy cows here. Bob Adams, however, had gotten shot for having an affair with one of his worker's wife. He had no heirs and his will stated the cattle were to be sold and the money to go to cancer research in memory of his own wife, who had died ten years earlier of colon cancer. The land was willed to the county, which had done nothing with it. Giant piles of manure were still there. Tommy pulled up to the farm.

He turned on the phone, made sure the pictures were on the memory card, then erased them from the phone's memory. Putting on work gloves, he wiped the phone off with his handkerchief. He put the phone in a zipper top plastic bag from his emergency kit and wiped off the plastic bag as well. Tommy got out of the cab of the truck and grabbed a long piece of pipe from the bed. He used the pipe to push the phone deep into a manure pile. He smiled to himself. Then he frowned, because it would not be nearly sufficient repayment for what had happened to Gregg.

He drove an indirect route back to the farm. He pulled into the barn and went to lie down. Tommy was suddenly exhausted. Michelle was sleeping deeply on the bottom bunk on the left side of the room, softly snoring.

Tommy looked out the small window. The sky had clouded up and a fine drizzle had begun to fall. Then he saw a military vehicle headed west in the direction of the Adams farm. Tommy told himself it was a coincidence. He did not really believe that, but he needed to sleep and didn't want to think of what it likely meant.

He sat down on the bunk opposite Michelle and watched her for a minute in the faint light coming in the window. He realized he might be able to love her. He didn't love her, but he might be able to. After his wife had died, that was something he never thought he would be able to consider .

He took off his shoes, lay down, and was asleep in minutes.

Chapter 14

Robert Braun woke after forty-five minutes when Hedwick knocked gently on the office door. He sat up quickly, feeling worse than he had when he had lay down. He was slightly lightheaded from the combination of the whisky and sitting up quickly.

"Yes?" He asked

"Cashman has located the phone. It is in the western part of the county. I've dispatched a team to retrieve it, and anyone they find with it. They should be there soon." She answered.

"Good."

"And Sue is set up to attempt initial contact with the object in the pit. She is just waiting for us."

"Good. Has medical figured out what happened to those two men?"

"Not yet. They are still completing the autopsies." Hedwick grimaced.

She was not weak and had killed when the job warranted. Hedwick had seen truly awful things. But there was something that deeply troubled her about the two men who had been killed by the thing. They were innocent. They had just been going about their work. Then they were dead.

Braun noticed the grimace, but let it go. He knew what was going through her mind. It had gone through his as well, but he also knew there was a job to do here, and sympathy or personal anguish would get in the way of doing that job effectively. The mess in Arizona had proven that.

"How soon?" Braun asked.

"The physical within the hour. Toxicology and pathology by noon tomorrow." She answered, glad to be thinking about details, instead of the implications the two deaths would have for the men's families.

The phone on the desk rang. Braun reached up from the sofa and answered it.

"Braun." he said.

He listened for a moment.

"Are you sure?... Well dig it out and bring it in." He hung up and let out a chuckle.

Hedwick looked at him, puzzled. "What could be funny in all of this?" she asked.

"Whoever had the phone, buried it in a pile of manure. Fowler wasn't happy about it. Serves him right, all the piles of crap I've gotten him out of over the years."

"It sounds like the person who had that phone knows the importance of that phone, and that we are looking for it. That makes things more difficult." Hedwick said.

"You're right. But not impossible." The smile left Braun's face as he got up from the sofa. He walked the length of the room, stretching as he walked, then retrieved the glass of whisky from the desk, and downed the remainder in a single swallow. That was all he would drink today.

"I need some coffee," he said. Coffee would have to suffice in place of sleep.

"There is some in the break room. I'll get it for you," she said.

"No, I'll get it myself. I need a change of scenery for a little while." He felt the air in the small office suddenly become stagnant, too warm and humid with the drizzle that had fallen while he had slept. The smell of his own sweat and the hot plastic of the sofa was stifling. There was another smell there as well. Robert could not put his finger on it. It was something earthy, musty and slightly acidic. He figured it had to do with the dampness. It was not unpleasant. At the same time it was a dark elemental smell. Robert instinctively knew it was something his lower brain would recognize. The break room, he knew, was air conditioned. He knew as well he would want the coolness of it when the whiskey really hit him.

Hedwick followed him out of the room. "I forgot to tell you, Fred Brandt did some rough calculations and based on the pictures of this thing we have and the size of the bit sticking out of the rock, he estimates it to be about 900 meters across, and all but about 10 meters are buried.

"900 meters," Braun said then let out a long, low whistle.

"That is, of course, if it has the same configuration as those we have seen before," she answered.

43

"The real question is whether or not it fused with the rock or displaced it. That answer will have to wait," he said.

They reached the coolness of the break room. Pouring coffee into a foam cup, he sat on a metal folding chair and stared into the depths of the coffee cup. Hedwig knew that look and knew he had retreated into his own mind to try and make sense of the events of the last day and a half. She left him alone. She had other things to take care of, while he processed.

Chapter 15

It was early twilight by the time Tommy woke. He could see Michelle was still sleeping. He was glad. He knew he would need her and, the more rested she was, the better. He felt refreshed himself. The images of Gregg's trailer flashed through his mind again. And once again he began to question whether it was really a good idea to try and find out what was going on. He wondered if maybe he should have just left the phone in the garbage. Of course it was too late for that. He knew he would never be able to forget what he had seen.

He wanted to wait until after dark to head toward the quarry and knew he had two choices. Neither was something he wanted to do, but he was sure he had to do something. He would run both options past Michelle. Maybe she could help him decide. After all, they were in this together.

He started to remember bits of a dream he had while he was sleeping. He remembered being on a spaceship. It was similar to ones he had seen in the movies he watched on Saturday afternoons on the TV when he was a kid. He was at the controls, but there was something wrong. The craft was crashing, and he could not do anything to stop it. Then he was standing on a strange planet with spongy ground. He was walking along a path with purple trees on both sides. Then it was gone. He guessed he was just trying to make sense of things.

"Michelle." He said. It was almost dark. It was time for her to wake up. She did not stir.

"Michelle." He said a bit louder. "It is time to wake up."

Michelle moaned quietly, then rolled over. She looked around for a moment before sitting up. It had taken her a minute to remember what had happened and where she was. She too felt more rested, but a little heady due to coming down from the Ritalin, with a bit of hangover from the Benadryl. This was why she used the Ritalin so rarely.

"What time is it?" She asked.

"Almost nine. Do you feel better?"

"A little. I had strange dreams. Not bad, just strange." She answered.

"Me too. Hold on a minute."

Tommy looked out the window. He untied a rope that was attached to a piece of wood that swung down over the outside of the window. Then he lowered a similar panel over the inside of the window. When he was sure the light would not be seen from outside, he flipped on the lamp that sat on a small table between the bunks. Tommy and his cousin had installed these panels for two reasons. The first was to block out the sun on Saturday mornings, the only day they got to sleep in. This was the explanation they gave their grandparents. The second, and more important, reason was to keep their grandparents from knowing how late they stayed up, especially on Friday nights.

"There, that should keep anyone from seeing the light." He said. He looked at her. He had turned the light on because he wanted to see her face as they talked.

"This isn't really the Army, is it?" She asked. She looked concerned. It was not fear that Tommy saw on her face, but a combination of confusion, sadness and anger. No Fear. That was good. He knew how to handle sadness, and quell anger, and together they could work on how to fix her confusion.

"Why do you say that?" Tommy asked. He had already come to the same conclusion, but he wanted to hear Michelle's thoughts. She may have noticed something or put their observations together in a way he had not.

"There are a couple things. They haven't let any media into the area. Radon, although dangerous, is not bad enough to keep them from having the media onsite to report. And, well, the Army doesn't kill people like Gregg. They might take them into custody, but they don't kill them outright. Before I slept I thought I could just walk away. But now, I know I can't. I have to know what is really going on. I'm just worried that when we get close enough to get some answers, we will end up like Gregg."

"Good, I agree totally with what you said. I also think they are going too far out of their way to totally clear the area around Shawnee. They could equip each house with a radon detector and provide regular health screenings for the residents at a tiny fraction of the cost of buying all that property. The value of the land alone for a two mile radius would be… Well, a two mile radius would make a circle of about twelve square miles, give or take. That would be about 7000 acres, at $3000 an acre would be twenty million just for the land. You add another 100 or so houses. We're talking thirty or forty million easy. I just don't think it adds up. It won't be long 'til someone else figures it out. I mean people live in houses all over here that have radon issues. There are ways to cut the risk to almost nothing. But, I have a feeling these people will have already created a deeper cover story if any questions come up." Tommy said.

"And there are the pictures. That is the clincher. No matter what else, that is what makes me think it is a cover up. "Michelle answered. The look of anger was becoming the dominant emotion Tommy saw in her eyes. He wasn't sure if that was a good thing. He could not recall ever seeing Michelle angry. Some people he knew used anger to their advantage, in a positive way. Others let it destroy them. He would have to watch this closely.

"We have two options as I see it. That is, if we are agreed that we can't walk away," Tommy said.

"I can't." Michelle answered.

"OK, the first option is to go to the quarry. We demand to see this Colonel Jackson and ask for answers." Tommy said. He paused. His face grew darker. "But, someone killed Gregg for what he knew. I don't like that option."

"Neither do I." she said softly. The anger in her eyes had slipped back to a look of fear.

"Or we can try to sneak in and see if we can get close enough to see what that thing is. I think we can get close, if we can go to my house. We act like I'm going to get my personal belongings. If they haven't figured out yet that we have the pictures, we have a chance."

Chapter 16

Hedwick Franklin sat at the computer terminal, cross checking the few images of the other, similar mystery objects against those of the thing in the pit. She had no doubt they were of the same origin. She also had no doubt they were different from what she had seen in Arizona.

The object in the pit and those other images showed curves. They had no linear surfaces. All the joints and surface transitions were gradual. The things in Arizona were not. They were sharp, almost boxy. They were reminiscent of the stealth bomber and F117 fighter. That, of course, made the cover-up in Arizona easy. The populations that saw them bought the idea that what they had seen were top secret, experimental aircraft, being developed as successors to those planes the public were already familiar with.

The thing in the pit was not like any craft originating on earth. If her calculations and those of her analysts were correct, there was nothing on earth that could even come close in size. There would be no "explaining away" of this thing. But that would only be a problem if reliable information about it got to the public.

"Ms. Franklin." A younger agent, named William James, stood in the doorway. Hedwick had not previously worked with him, but knew his dossier. He was, perhaps, smarter than anyone on the team, but gave the impression of being not particularly creative. When assigned a problem, he was fast to solve it, but often made it appear that he was unable to see the problem for himself. Hedwick did not completely buy the facade. She knew he was a lot more on the ball than he let on. She was not sure of his motivation. The brilliance of his solutions to complex problems made her feel that he was hiding something. He was a valuable asset no doubt, but he had to be carefully managed to keep him on track.

"Yes Billy?" She used his nickname intentionally to reaffirm the fact of being his superior.

"The phone has been recovered. That is the good news." He said.

He paused.

"And the bad news?" Hedwick obligingly asked. She had a sudden flash of half a dozen movies, where a similar scene had been played out. She hated cliché, but knew she had to pretend to play with William. She justified this game to herself as "using people skills."

"The bad news is that the memory card has been removed. Whatever that phone had on it, is still out there." William answered.

"And just what did that phone have on it?" It was a game for William, but for her it was like getting cavities filled. She hated this cat and mouse stupidity. Why could William not just give her all the information, without pulling teeth? "People skills" she again reminded herself.

"The computer guys are working on that right now. They expect to have recovered at least the last thing transferred to the card in the next thirty minutes. And the initial autopsy results are complete. Those guys had two things that happened simultaneously, either of which would have been fatal. The first was a full body burn that doc says looks like an electrical burn. It charred the skin and likely stopped the heart. They had third degree burns over 99% of their bodies. Enough charge to cause this burn almost certainly would have fried their nervous system. The second thing was that their internal organs, including their brains, were liquefied. The doc seems to think it was maybe due to some sort of ultrasonic vibration, but he isn't sure of that. He says it is just a theory."

"So it was pretty much instanteous, in other words? Thank goodness for small favors. What is the story we are going to tell the families of those workers?"

"The plan was to say they were assisting us with the initial assessment of the situation, and there was an explosion due to an additional pocket of natural gas we encountered." William answered.

"That seems a bit thin." Hedwick said.

"Not really. Natural gas is produced in the area. And the pit has had shutdowns before because of encounters with it—usually small pockets between layers of limestone. There has never been an explosion, but in 1994 there was a fire. So it is not unheard of. We can say they were tired and overworked and under a lot of stress and even list it as human error due to unfamiliarity with equipment. I'll have Jansen work up the story for your approval in the next hour or two."

Hedwick knew Jansen would not have anything to do with the story, other than to deliver it. William would already have all the details in his head. He would simply tell Jansen what to tell the families and the press. It was just another part of the game. Hedwick knew that. But she knew it would be pointless to say anything to William, and probably make it impossible to get full benefit of his talents, if he became defensive.

"Good. Keep me posted." She rose and left the office. She had nowhere specific to go. She was playing the final card in the game, to yet again show who was in charge.

Chapter 17

William James watched Hedwick walk out of the office, a little smile curling at the corners of his mouth. The last few minutes had gone exactly to plan. He had played his game and Hedwick had played hers. Now William knew exactly where he stood and how far he could push. He also had learned that there was no suspicion of his real agenda.

This thing in the quarry was what he had been waiting for. He had been trying for years to be in a place where he might get his hands on enough concrete evidence to expose at least a portion of what was being hidden from the public.

He had grown up with a Libertarian father who very much wanted transparency in government. William's father had disappeared in the early 1990's after he discovered information about some unsanctioned (at least not officially recognized) operations in the oil fields of Kuwait. He had been a contractor who had signed on to help replace the well heads after the fires had been put out. During his time there, he had been contacted by some individuals who had claimed to be representatives of the well owners. They had asked him to cap a portion of the wells, and say they were burned out instead of placing a take off head on them. He later found out, through a drunken military officer at a local bar, that the reason was to artificially reduce output, and drive up the price of crude oil.

When his father had disappeared, William already knew enough to play innocent and ignorant. It had served him well. The man who had recruited William had teased him in with the simple question: "Would you like to know what really happened to your father?"

William had a good idea of what had happened. He continued to play innocent to see how far he could get into the background operations and hidden agendas most people did not know existed.

He was amazed when he had been told the truth about what had happened to his father. His father had been given a choice of voluntarily disappearing, or being forcibly "disappeared". His father had chosen the first option. As far as William knew he was still living in Seattle and working at the Space Needle. William had been able to confirm he was still alive with his own eyes shortly after he began to work with the organization.

William realized his father had failed for one simple reason: trying to expose something without irrefutable evidence. That is where William had taken a much longer term approach. He had wanted to exonerate and, in a way, avenge his father. William wanted to expose the same behind the scenes, covert things that were still going on. He felt felt that, to do so, would require evidence that was completely bulletproof. That thing in the pit, if he played this right, would be that evidence.

William reflected on why he was doing this. He thought about how he had always believed in the power of honesty. About the time he was five or six-years-old, he had been highly troubled any time he found out he had not been told the truth.

He remembered when he found out that Santa Clause was not real. It was devastating. His own parents, the people he had trusted implicitly his entire life, had been lying to him. He took a long look at what honesty meant to him. He thought about it deeply—at least as deeply as a six-year-old can. He decided then that honesty was the most important part of any relationship.

This faith in honesty had been the driving force behind why he was trying to expose the covert, hidden things of the world. It was this belief in the power of honesty that more than once nearly cost him his current position. He walked a fine line of trying always to tell the truth without disclosing any information that would damage his position. He never had lied, although he often did omit bits of truth in his own best interest.

He thought about the last time he had not told the whole truth in response to a direct question. It had left him stranded alongside a dirt road in the desert outside Las Vegas. But, had he told all of the pertinent information he knew, he would be dead. Of that he had no doubt. It was easy to withhold information when it is not directly asked for. It was something else entirely to "not lie" creatively, and still not give the sought after information. This was a skill that William had honed over many years. He was proud that he had not ever had to resort to any existential trickery to be able to do it either. He did not feel it was consistent with what he believed truth really means. Occasionally he did think long and hard to come up with an appropriate semantic trick to achieve his ends. But he had not ever directly told a lie.

During a conversation once in college, William had described his beliefs to one of his friends.

"Honesty is the only means by which one can be totally self-consistent in their life. Any time someone lies, no matter how noble the reason," (one of William's friends had argued that it was acceptable to lie in a situation where it would achieve a good greater than the damage caused by the lie), "or how small the lie, there becomes an inconsistency in the person's psyche. They know they have lied, and that there is a possibility of that lie being discovered. If one is committed to only telling the truth, there is never that possibility. If the person is not usually given to lies, the untruth will torment them. If the person is prone to lying frequently, unless they are very good, they have likely been discovered in their lies, and when they do tell the truth, they will not be believed. Honesty is the most self-consistent means of assuring oneself of always being believed, and to not have to bear the torment of having lied in the first place."

Hand in hand with William's belief in the power of honesty, was his belief in trust. Later in the same conversation he said, "Honesty is only one part of it though. Trust is the other part. It does no good for the hearer to be told the truth, if they do not believe it. But if a person is trusted, in addition to that person being honest, that is a great combination. Trusting someone is probably the best loyalty one can show another person. To be called heroic or courageous is wonderful, but to be trusted is perhaps, for me at least, the best compliment I could be paid. I would rather be poor and powerless and trusted, than wealthy and powerful, but be constantly under suspicion."

After a couple minutes of mulling over these things, William shook himself. He knew that he was on the precipice, looking down into darkness. He knew that if he succeeded in getting evidence of the operation and the cover-up to the public his whole life would change, and he did not know how. For now he decided that he could not be concerned with that. He had much to do, and it must be done quickly. He left the small office and headed to the room where the computer guys were set up, trying to retrieve the images that had been deleted from the phone.

Chapter 18

"Before we try this, we need some more information." Tommy said.

"And I need to put in an appearance at the paper or someone there will be suspicious from that direction too. Besides, that likely will be the best source of information we will have access to. I don't expect to learn anything beyond the 'official story', but some of the details of that might be useful." Michelle said.

"I agree," Tommy said. "There is something else that came to mind. Where is your car? Did you leave it somewhere it will raise suspicion?"

"No, it's at home, in the garage. I caught a ride to the school with Terry Prop. He lives a couple doors over. He works for the radio station." Michelle answered.

"Good. How do we explain what you have been up to for the last sixteen hours?"

"I'll just say I'm working on a story about the evacuation, and that you have been helping me with a first hand account from the viewpoint of one of the evacuees."

"That will work. How soon will the story have to be turned in?" Tommy asked.

"Anytime before noon tomorrow should keep the wolves from the door."

"Okay. Tonight I want to drive around the perimeter of the evacuation zone. I want to get a feel for how many personnel we are looking at, and how they are setting up the access points. Tomorrow you can go to the paper and gather the rest of the information we'll need, before we try and get close to that thing." Tommy said.

They lapsed into silence; both deep in thought. Tommy's stomach made an audible growling sound. Michelle looked at him, at first with a look of disbelief, then with a big smile.

"Sounds like you need some food. Come to think of it, I could use some too. How about the B & Z over in Axiom? Being seen together would lend some credence to our cover." Michelle said.

"Sounds like a good idea. By the time we're done, it will be full dark and we can go on our reconnoiter."

They drove to the B&Z and ordered. The B&Z was an old school root beer drive in, complete with carhops on roller skates. It had been in operation since the 1950's, one of the few businesses still thriving in the little town. Tommy's cousin, Shad, was two stalls over on the opposite side. Tommy thought that was good.

"I'll go plant some seeds of our cover story with him. He knows everyone and likes to talk. Do you wanna come?" Tommy asked.

"Sure. I need to hear what you tell him to keep our stories straight," Michelle answered. "Besides, we have a few minutes 'til the food will be ready."

They got out and went to Shad's truck.

"Tommy boy! How are you doing? Are you part of the evacuation? I know you are close over there," Shad said.

"Yep, I was wondering if your dad had any food out at the cabin. I was planning on staying out there tonight. I figure I'll go to the house in the morning and get a few things," Tommy said.

"I think there is some canned stuff out there, and there is a little venison in the freezer from last season. There's nothing fresh, but you could get by a day or two. How long you planning on staying out there?"

"Just a few days. Just 'til I figure out where I'm gonna stay permanently. Would you mind letting your dad know? My cell phone is dead, and I left the charger at the house," Tommy said.

"Oh sure. Are you going to be staying alone?" Shad asked under his breath, with a glance toward Michelle and a wink toward Tommy.

"Yes." Tommy answered. "She is working on a story for the paper, and apparently I'm 'public interest'." He gave Shad a wink back with the eye that Michelle could not see.

"I don't see it." Shad said. He chuckled. "Hey, it looks like your food is out. I'll let Dad know you're gonna be staying at the cabin. Let me know if I can do anything for you."

"Thanks Shad. I'll check the salt licks while I'm out there." Tommy said.

Michelle did not say anything while they walked back to the truck. Once they were inside the truck she said, "Did you know we used to date? He is still a piece of work. Once a shmoe, always a shmoe I guess." She smiled.

"I know. He told stories about you back in high school. I'm sure none of them are true," Tommy said.

"Well, maybe a few are true." She said. Now she winked at Tommy.

Tommy blushed.

Chapter 19

Robert looked down the long hallway leading to the cement plant's employee parking lot. He could see the air shimmer from the heat rising off the asphalt outside. Even though the sun was setting, Robert knew it was going to be hot outside. He hated the heat. It made him feel as if some unseen hound from hell was breathing down his neck. It was especially uncomfortable in the humid hot of the Midwest. In some ways it was worse after the sun went down, because the heat and humidity did not end. All the heat that had been absorbed during the day, by the roads and fields, maintained the heat, long after sunset, and any decrease in temperature would mean the relative humidity would rise. With the humidity high, it was a double curse: one would get drenched in their own sweat and not be able to get cool.

He had spent years here, on and off, with various assignments. He understood the summers here, but still detested them. This heat was different from the heat in Arizona. There it was hot but dry. Here the slightest exertion resulted in dripping sweat, and clinging clothes.

He was hypnotized by the shimmer of the air outside the window. His mind wandered to the summer of 1988, when he had been in Columbus in August. The temperature was between ninety-five and one hundred degrees with the humidity in the ninety percent range. That was one of his first jobs with the agency, when he actually did the work in the field. It was not like now when he directed others to do the dirty work. It was the first time he had been shot at, other than with the rubber bullets used in training. It was also the first time he had killed another human. He could remember the absolute silence of everything after the last gunshot. Everything had been still, except for the subtle waving of the air, and the thunder rumbling in the distance with the monster thunderstorm that would break the bonfire heat wave.

He snapped back to the present, as Hedwick rounded the corner from an adjoining hallway into his line of sight. She had recognized the far away look on his face and knew she had caught him off guard. She walked slowly—or at least slower than she usually did—to allow Robert a moment to pull himself back from wherever he had gone mentally. She did not remember him having moments like this the last time that they had worked together. It did not bother her, but she decided it was a detail she needed to pay attention to. Lack of attention at the wrong moment could be fatal, and even though she no longer loved him, she did still care for him. He was an essential asset to the agency.

"Sue is ready for us in the pit," Hedwick said when she felt his attention had returned to the moment.

"Good. What is the approach plan?" Robert asked.

Hedwick approached him and pointed to the aerial photo on her clipboard. "There is a limestone wall here, where they have set up a surveillance cage. It is out to the line of sight from the object. The location of the cage gives about 100 feet of limestone between us and the object. The initial approach will be done by BARRy. We will decide on further approach strategies based on what the scanners show."

The Ballistic Armored Reconnaissance Robot was a steel and Kevlar shielded conglomeration of electronics and firearms on tank treads. There were cameras to provide a 360° view from ground to zenith. There are also sensors for infrared, radio, microwave, x-ray and UV radiation. Initially the ballistic in 'BARRy' was an adjective referring to the armor. It had been Robert's idea to add weaponry several years ago, after losing an agent who had been out numbered. The few times BARRy had been used in an offensive situation, those on whom the guns had been targeted gave up without shots being fired. There was something psychologically intimidating about a robot with a gun, even if it was a person at the controls.

"Good. What kind of readings are we getting off it right now?" Robert asked.

They started walking down the hallway in the opposite direction from the parking lot. They passed the time clock.

"That is the thing. We are getting no readings," she answered.

At this Robert stopped. He turned to her and gave her a single raised eyebrow.

"What exactly does 'no readings' mean?" He looked past here to the time clock: 21:31. For some reason the number struck a bell. The connection did not come to his mind immediately and he forgot it almost as quickly as it had come.

"Just that. The equipment is functioning exactly as it should. There are no electromagnetic waves coming off that thing except visible light. That isn't a problem. The problem is that within 50 yards of that thing there are no radio, television, microwave or other signals at all. There is a 50,000 watt transmission tower for one of the local radio stations 9 miles from here. There should be at least that signal. That thing is absorbing everything with a wavelength."

"Do any of the tech guys have any ideas?" Robert asked.

"Not really. But we have decided to send BARRy in with a tether, just in case." They began walking again. When they reached the end of the hallway they went out the door on the quarry side of the building. They squinted in the brightness of the remnants of sunset for a few moments. A few hundred feet ahead of them was the object. They paused for a moment, then walked on in silence.

Chapter 20

Tommy and Michelle ate their dinner as Tommy outlined his plan.

"I think we should circle around north of the river, 'til we get to the far side of Shawnee. We can cross at the Bethel Bridge. Once we are near the perimeter we can go around to the south and circle the quarry. I think that should give us a pretty good idea of how much manpower is being used to secure the area," Tommy said.

"Okay, that sounds good. After we finish the loop, we should go to my house and get some rest, as soon as we finish figuring out what to do." Michelle said. She took a long pull on her Mountain Dew milkshake, then got a worried expression.

"What is that look for?" Tommy asked.

"I was just thinking…about Gregg. Wondering if we should change vehicles. If they are looking for you, they will know what you're driving," she answered.

"Yeah. I thought about that. But, we've already established that you and I are spending time together. If they are looking for me, they are looking for you too."

"I was thinking more along the lines of not letting them see your truck patrolling their perimeters," Michelle said.

Tommy thought for a moment. He took a long pull on his root beer. That had not occurred to him. He had not thought that far into the vehicle thing. He was a little disturbed that he hadn't. Any mistake right now could be very dangerous.

"That's a good point," he finally said. "I think there is a solution. Did you see the old Chevelle in the barn?"

"No, I didn't," Michelle said with a raised eyebrow.

"Shad actually has the title to it, but all the cousins chip in to keep up the registration and the insurance. So any of us can use it if we need an extra vehicle, or we have one in the shop. That car wouldn't trace back to me, even if they did check plates," Tommy said.

"That would work. So we need to swing by there first. We can hide your truck there too."

"I think it may be a good idea to hide your car there as well," Tommy said.

"I suppose it is. Or maybe leave it where it is. I'm starting to wonder if I should even go to work," Michelle said.

"Let's decide that when we see what things look like around the Quarry," Tommy said.

They finished their meal in silence. Tommy reached out and pushed the button for the carhop to come and take the garbage. When he looked back at Michelle, he saw her staring straight through the windshield, her eyes enormous. Tommy followed her gaze.

There was a big military vehicle pulled up in front of the stand. A giant of a man with sergeant's insignia got out. He strode to the carry out window. Tommy held his breath.

"What can I getcha?" the girl at the window asked.

The man unfolded a piece of paper, and began to read off a large order for burgers, fries, chili dogs and other food. Tommy exhaled. The carhop arrived, and took their tray. Tommy rolled up his window and started the truck as calmly as possible.

After he had driven about half a block from the stand, he looked at Michelle and said, "That was too close for my taste."

"Mine too. Let's go get the Chevelle and just forget my car," Michelle said.

They drove to the barn, making sure they were not followed. After parking the truck in the barn, they pulled out in the Chevelle and began their reconnaissance. The encounter at the root beer stand had brought home how dangerous the situation really was.

Chapter 21

Robert and Hedwick walked across the fifty yards from the main building to the ramp that led down into the pit. The space between the building and the pit was paved with gravel. The crunch of it as they walked reminded Robert of the crunch of tires on gravel roads. It was one of the few distinct memories he had prior to the age of five. He often remembered sitting in the back seat of his mother's Chevy with the windows down on a cool fall day. The brilliant yellow, red and brown leaves had started falling from the maples and cottonwoods that grew in the ditches along the country roads leading to his grandmother's house.

Robert was going to be staying with his grandmother for the weekend while his mother went to pick up his father at the airport after a long business trip. His parents had never made it back to pick him up from his grandmother's house. The car wreck happened just a couple miles from where they would have turned off the highway onto those crunchy, gravel, back roads.

As Robert and Hedwick began the walk down into the pit, Robert was stunned by two things. The first was the size of the pit. The far side was rapidly disappearing into the dimness of twilight. He noticed it was almost impossible to grasp the scale of things. There was little to provide perspective. On another ramp on the north side of the pit was a dump truck that looked like a toy. Robert knew this was an illusion . He had stood next to a similar truck that was parked near the office building and could not see over the top of the tires.

The second thing that struck him was the silence. This was perhaps due to the constant clank and jingle and whine of the ancient air conditioning in the office building he had become used to. More likely, it was due to the scale of the pit which muffled sounds amongst the gravel and dust. Once they had descended past the rim of the pit, all the sounds from above the surface disappeared.

The only distinct sound Robert could identify was the basso

profundo croaking of a solitary bullfrog from the pond at the bottom of the oldest part of the pit. The water from the pond was used to cool the drills that bored into the limestone. The long drills cut deep holes into the rocks which were packed with explosives. When the explosives were detonated, the blast would break the stone into huge blocks. Robert suddenly was saddened by that frog. He was not sure why. All the same, he knew there would possibly be one more blast here to bury that thing if they ultimately determined it posed any kind of danger. That had been the contingency plan from the start. They could easily claim that the blast would seal off the radon leak.

The ramp they walked down was thirty feet wide, a shallow grade meant to allow the heaviest trucks to negotiate it even when fully loaded with stone. About 100 yards along, there was a switchback that made a huge arc to accommodate those same trucks. After the third switchback, the ramp leveled out onto a wide plateau within the pit. There were two of the massive dump trucks here and a large front loader that had been abandoned when the object, now only a few hundred feet away, appeared. The equipment had stopped working, no coughing or sputtering, it had just stopped.

They looped around the left side of the plateau to come up behind the outcropping of rock that would be their shielding. The distance to the cage was almost 500 feet, yet it seemed closer because of the vast scale of the rest of the pit. The quarry operation had originally begun on a 100 acre plot. Soon after the quality of the stone and the very deep water table were discovered, Shawnee had purchased nearly four square miles of farm land. The current pit covered just half of the available area.

As they walked the last few yards to the cage, the stars above began to pop out. Robert looked up and saw tiny points of light: blue and yellow, red and green—but none were truly white. Robert thought about the scene at the end of "Men in Black" where Tommy Lee Jones muses about being unable to just "look at the stars" any more, because he knew too much. Robert understood that feeling. But, unlike the movie there was no device to make him forget what he knew. And if there was, he would not have wanted to use it.

They reached the cage. It was a cube with the side furthest from the object and the floor open. The other four sides were heavy duty aluminum frames with thick, twelve foot squares of a laminated polycarbonate that could withstand a bazooka blast.

The wall closest to the object also had two large panels of lead sandwiched between sheets of stainless steel. Behind one of these panels were the computers and other sensitive electronics in a ground-to-roof rack. The other lead panel was reserved for shielding the human occupants of the cage.

Although the cage was twelve feet high, there was only about seven feet of headroom. The upper portion was occupied by additional electronics, each with its own heavy shielding. There was also a generator, fuel tanks and batteries to supply the power to the electronics and lights.

Just in front of the cage was BARRy. The robot often reminded Robert of the Daleks on the old Dr WHO TV reruns he had watched on PBS as a teen. On the back, attached to a ring welded to the chassis, was a half inch thick steel and carbon fiber cable. The other end of the cable was attached to a winch—the control to which were inside the cage—with the cable threaded through a hole in the polycarbonate. This was a recent addition, Robert noted. He wondered how long it had taken to drill that hole, and what special hardened bit had been required.

"So, is everything ready?" Robert asked.

"Yes, sir. Just waiting on your go," answered Sue Carter, the tech who had built BARRy. She was in charge of all the computers and other electronic hardware onsite. Sue was an enigmatic blend of state of the art and old school. At once, she could quote the latest research on quantum computing, fuzzy logic and holographic memory storage, and be building an analog circuit using tubes and relays. She was just as comfortable with a laptop as a slide rule. She possessed the ability to think digitally or in analogies of flowing water or dropping stones, depending on what was required to solve a particular problem.

Her appearance was even more of a puzzle than her mind. She could alternately seem thirty or sixty-years-old, or anywhere in between. Her hair, over the last five years had been no less than twelve different colors, from a light blue-green to jet black. Currently it was an iridescent shade of her own devising that showed varying shades from green to purple, depending on how the light hit it. Her eyes were stunning. Her right eye was cobalt blue and her left sea foam green. Her ethnicity, as well, was impossible to determine. Some who saw her said Asian, others Middle Eastern, still others

Slavic, depending on the expression on her face. Most of the time that expression, to an outsider who was unaware of her keen mind, was that of someone in a stupor or stoned. In reality, she wore that expression when she was most focused. She was attractive when she wanted to be, which was infrequently. When she was, as she was at that moment, excited and in a state of full animation, she looked her youngest and most stunning.

Sue had been with the agency since the beginning. She knew more and had seen more than Robert could have imagined. She had briefed presidents and been loaned to various legitimate government agencies as a consultant on all things electronic. One would never know these things to look at her, which was just as she wished.

"What is the approach plan?" Robert asked.

"We'll send BARRy in along the wall to this point," Sue said, pointing to a spot on a monitor that was out of view from the cage. "Then we'll cut in at an angle to come straight to this point." She pointed to another monitor where the object and limestone met. "If everything goes well, then we will take readings and see what we can see." She flipped a switch and four more monitors came on.

"The robot's cameras will be displayed on these 3 monitors and on this one will be the scanner read outs."

"Everything looks good, you have my go," said Robert.

Sue typed a few keystrokes into the keyboard to her left. When she pressed "enter", BARRy began to roll away from the cage.

Chapter 22

Michelle looked through the windshield of the Chevelle as she and Tommy drove east. She watched the deepening twilight in the rearview mirror and the growing shadows in the corn and bean fields. They passed a wheat field where straw was being baled, late in the season.

This was Rolland Mowery's field. Michelle was temporarily distracted by a story she had been assigned a couple months before. She had finished the story just before the assignment that put her in the Chevelle with Tommy. Rolland had been a classmate of Michelle and always knew he would take over the family farm. He was the oldest son of Frank and Ruby Mowery, who were themselves third generation on the farm. Ruby died shortly after the boys had graduated from high school. Frank had died the previous spring. He had been one of the few farmers who had been able to thrive, even while many other family farms in the county had gone under.

After Frank had died, the will was read and, as expected, the farm was left to Rolland. Despite the clear directive, the farm was tied up in probate, including the crops, until just last week. Rolland and his brothers had been working around the clock trying to catch up. It was too late to plant beans after the wheat. Rolland was going to miss an entire crop. He would likely struggle for a couple years to catch up, simply because his father died at the wrong time of year. Had Frank died earlier, Rolland would be able to double crop; later in the year and the wheat would have already been harvested, and the beans would be in in the ground.

Michelle thought about how timing can play a critical role in how events unfold. How a single instant can totally change the course of the future. If she had not been a little late to the news conference, she would have gotten a better place, closer to the front. She would not have been near the door and seen Tommy drop the phone into the trash. She would not be here in this car.

She was brought back to the present when Tommy pulled into

the Orange Owl, a convenience store that looked out over the river very near the Bethel Bridge.

"What kind of phone do you have, and does it have a camera?" Tommy asked.

"It does. It is a smartphone. Why?" Michelle answered.

"Do you have a charger? If not, we need to get one," Tommy said.

"No, my wall charger is at home and my car charger…well, you know," she said.

"Sandy has a lot of cell stuff. And, if he doesn't have a charger, I'll bet he has a cheap digital camera. Come on, let's see what we can find," Tommy said.

They went into the store. Like Rolland Mowery, Sandy Goodrich was fourth generation in the convenience store. Originally it had been called "The Lighthouse" because of the forty foot tower that once stood on the east end of the building. The tower had been struck by lighting and burned to the ground twenty years ago. Everyone still called the Orange Owl "The Lighthouse".

Sandy was a big man. He spent too much time alone with the potato chips and snack cakes that lined the shelves of the store. He was his own best customer. He carried it well on his seventy-four inch frame, holding much of the weight in his legs, due to being on his feet all day. The Owl was open from 9am 'til 10pm, seven days a week. Sandy was always there. He lived in the small house attached to the back of the store. It was understood that, if Sandy had to leave, the store would close.

Sandy smiled as they came through the door. "Tommy! Long time, no see," he said sarcastically. Tommy stopped frequently to buy beer and shoot the breeze.

"Hi. Sandy, do you have a changer for a smartphone? I ran over Michelle's," Tommy said.

"Oh, hi, Michelle. It really has been a while. What model phone you got? I've got one for the M-6 and a couple for the M-9," Sandy said.

"I've got an M-9," Michelle said.

"No problem," Sandy said. He reached under the counter and pulled out the charger. "Anything else?"

"Maybe one of those prepaid phones. My cell is on the fritz. I had it in my shirt pocket and it dropped into the toilet when I bent over to flush," Tommy said.

"Eww. You aren't the first. I've got a basic one for $19.95 plus minutes. Will that do? I assume you had insurance on the other phone?" Sandy asked. He knew Tommy did not. Sandy had discussed the issue with Tommy before. He gave Michelle a wink.

"You know I don't, Sandy. Besides my contract was up anyway. I'll take one of those cheap phones and 100 minutes." Tommy said.

"No problem. You're lucky I've got any left. One of the military guys from over at Shawnee came in and bought about twenty of 'em. And cards for about 5000 minutes. He said that the phones they had were for military use only, and several of the guys' personal phones didn't work here. He said they all had some carrier I'd never heard of that was local to the Fort Deatrick area. I didn't ask too many questions after he put a few Bennies on the counter. And I wasn't thinking about asking too many anyway. I think Jim Croce said it best; 'If you looked deep enough into his eyes, you could see the back of his skull,' and well, I'm hoping they keep me in mind if they need any more creature comforts. Okay, the phone, minutes and charger come up to $35.19."

Tommy grabbed a couple sodas from the case next to the registers and handed over two twenties. "Thanks, Sandy. Keep it. And let me know if you hear anything interesting from those Army guys. My house is in the evacuation zone and I'm curious for any info I can get that doesn't come through official channels."

"Give me a minute to get this phone activated for you. And since you mentioned it, the guy who came in for the phones did say something to his buddy about being sure to have these all turned off when they were in the quarry. I thought that was strange. If there is radon in the pit wouldn't they stay out of there unless they were in hazard suits anyway? But, like I said, I didn't hear too much once Mr. Franklin started talking."

"They probably don't want to take a chance of setting off any explosions. There was a blast scheduled for tomorrow. As fast as the workers were cleared out they may have left some goodies in the pit. It would be bad form to bury your comrades because of talking to your girlfriend," Tommy said.

"I hadn't thought about that. Okay, the phone is ready." Sandy said.

"Thanks. And you obviously have the number if you hear

anything," Tommy said and started to head out.

"Sure thing. Have a good one."

"Good night, Sandy," Michelle said. She and Tommy walked out and got into the car. They headed toward the Bethel Bridge in silence, both lost in their own thoughts.

Finally Michelle asked, "What do they need the phones for?"

"I don't know, but it isn't for checking in with the ball and chain. I bet it has everything to do with them being untraceable." Tommy said.

Chapter 23

Robert Braun stood against the shield in the front of the cage, where he could simultaneously watch through the narrow observation slit in the shielding and see the monitors showing the view from BARRy's cameras. He was silent. He knew that there would be little useful incoming information until the robot rounded the end of the rock wall. That would likely be in about five minutes. It would take a while for Sue to run a total check on the controls and telemetry, before she sent it around the corner. Robert was watching the same shimmer he had seen earlier, rising up from the depths of the pit. His mind again wandered to that blistering summer in Columbus.

That had been a summer of firsts for Robert: his first assignment, his first kill, his first time being shot at. It had also been the first time he had understood that he could not allow himself to fall in love. The consequences could be too dangerous. He had long since, as a means to deal with his loneliness, classified those dangers into three categories.

It was a list that he often ran over in his mind, and did again as he grew acutely aware of Hedwick standing close to him, so as to have a view to correspond to his. The first danger was that love colored all decisions. It could be used as leverage by an opponent in critical situations. The second was that love can put innocent persons in danger, namely the object of love. The third, and this was the greatest motivator to Robert, was that of love being able to cause excruciating pain. Love lost, either by love leaving, or the object of love being destroyed, had resulted in such pain for Robert that summer, that he had developed his three principles as a shield against ever being prey to those dangers again. He had been a fan of Isaac Asimov's Robot stories, and likened his three laws of love to the three laws of robotics. The analogy might have seemed poor to some, but he held on to it anyway.

"I'm ready," Sue said.

Robert looked from the slit in the shield to the monitors.

"Good. Let's go. Send it around the corner," Robert said.

"Okay. Here we go. I'll set all the readouts to zero to compensate for baseline," Sue said. She typed a few keystrokes. There was a beep and several of the lines on the monitors jumped then settled to a steady, even level.

Robert looked back through the slit in the shielding and watched BARRy approach the corner of the limestone wall. As the robot rolled past the edge of the wall, out of his sight and into the line of sight of the object, Robert looked back at the monitors. The view almost took his breath away.

Robert had thought he had been prepared for the size of the thing. But he had not really been prepared. He did not have—and none of them had—anything in their experience to prepare them for the scale of the thing. He shook himself mentally.

"Are we getting anything off it other than the visible light we are seeing?" Robert asked.

"No. In the UV, radio, microwave and infrared it shows up as a hole; a complete lack of anything." Sue answered. She pointed to the two monitors where there was a black profile of the object. "It doesn't emit, but it also doesn't reflect. And if you notice, the profile is larger than the visual of the object. All theses monitors are set to the same scale."

Robert looked from monitor to monitor, and was surprised that the hole appeared to be about a third larger than the visible light image.

"Why do you suppose that would be, Sue?" he asked.

"There are a couple possibilities that come to mind, but I'm not even sure how to begin to put it coherently. It is more of a feeling of what might be going on," Sue answered.

Robert knew this was how she analyzed complex situations. The solution would begin as a feeling. She would use this feeling to guide a few experiments or give rise to a question or two. It was the results of these experiments or the answer to the questions that would crystallize, completely formed, the explanation for any given phenomenon. This ability had caused some friction with her professors at college and in grad school. They believed that every solution to every problem should begin with first principles and proceed from there in a logical stepwise fashion. She was often able with her intuition and a page of calculations to answer in a few minutes complex questions her fellow students took days and a dozen pages to accomplish.

"The simplest explanation, please. If you have one," Robert said.

"The only way I can account for seeing visual and no other wavelengths is that somehow the object is absorbing all frequencies. At the same time it is generating a visual image of itself. Or there are other possibilities involving harmonics and wave particle duality that I'm still trying to work out." Sue said.

"How far 'til where it seems all the radiation disappears?" Hedwick asked.

"We'll come up to that in about fifty feet. My guess is that nothing will happen," Sue said.

They watched. Hedwick saw the cable on the tether play out slowly. Sue watched the monitors. Robert watched the point where the tether cable rounded the outcropping. The cable bit slowly into the rock causing a snowfall of fine powdered rock dust. It reminded Robert of the winter there in the Midwest. It seemed a strange juxtaposition to him, thinking about snow in the hot plastic box.

"Almost there. Ten feet," Sue said.

"Five."

"Four."

Three.

Two."

"One."

The robot rolled forward for about a second after Sue said "one," then the monitors all went black. The robot stopped responding completely.

"Hmm. That's interesting. I guess I was right. This just wasn't the nothing I was expecting," Sue said.

Chapter 24

William sat down at the computer terminal. There was no window in the room and the monitor faced away from the door, so he was not worried about anyone seeing what he was doing. It really would not matter if someone did see. Still he would prefer to not have to make any explanations. He was simply watching and listening to the feed from the bug he had placed in the cage. He had installed it while he was helping Sue unload the cage from the truck. William was confident the bug remained undetected. Its signal was piggybacked on the regular signals coming out of the cage.

He clicked in a few keystrokes to launch the recording program that would send a copy of the feed to a USB drive stuck into the front of the machine. William looked down to be sure the drive was working. He was satisfied to see the flashing yellow-green glow that reminded him of the fireflies he used to see outside his bedroom windows on summer nights when he was growing up.

For the moment, there was not much going on in the cage. Sue was there but Hedwick and Robert had not yet arrived. He could not stay to watch. There were other things to which he had to attend. He was sure he would be able to come back and watch if something exciting happened. He typed in a few more keystrokes and heard the audio feed in his earpiece. He knew he could listen, at least, to what was going on out there while he took care of some other loose ends.

He left the room after placing a small device under the front lip of the door. It was something he had designed himself in high school, and tweaked to its present form. Essentially it was a small mercury switch coupled with a tiny transmitter. Any movement of the door would trigger the switch and the transmitter would send a subtle, repeating alarm to William's earpiece. This was a simple device, but it was one he had not mentioned to his coworkers. He felt that, even in a world of cloak and dagger, he needed to have a few secrets of his own.

He opened the door as a test. The signal beeped in his ear. He closed the door and reset the device.

William walked down the hall to where the computer gurus were working on the phone.

"So, what do we have?" he asked.

"Well, so far we have pulled off four images. The file handling on this thing is pretty primitive. I had to hack the firmware to get at it. This is a case of older tech being harder to hack than the newer stuff. Anyway it looks like there were a total of 7 files transferred to the memory card at about the same time. Because of the memory sharing set up...," Sid Sharp, the lead technogenius said. He was cut short by William.

"I understand that you find this all fascinating, but cut the jargon and please show me the pictures you have so far." He said.

"Oh...okay" Sid said.

Sid was socially awkward. He preferred to spend time with the machines than with people. William knew this and knew that the technospeak was part of Sid's coping mechanism for dealing with other people. William had cut Sid off on purpose. He knew if he had not, Sid would have gone on perpetually, explaining in further and more minute detail what he had done to recover the pictures, and in excruciating detail what he would do to obtain the remaining photos.

After a moment in which Sid had to stop and consciously process what William had said, he typed in a couple keystrokes and four photos appeared on the monitor. Each picture took up a quarter of the screen. There were two pictures of the dead quarry workers. The third picture was a blurry shot of part of the object.

The fourth image caught William's eye. There was the object, but this picture was taken from a different angle than the other photo. The image was much sharper.

"Can you make that one fill the screen?" William asked, pointing to the fourth photo.

"Sure," Sid said. He had regained his equilibrium and had immediately started typing. The picture filled the screen.

William saw what appeared as almost a halo around the object. Near one edge of the object there was a truck in the background. The image of the truck appeared to be smashed out—spread out, it appeared—on the surface of the object.

"Zoom in there." William said and pointed to the spot where the truck appeared flattened.

The image quickly became pixelated. By squinting William saw the truck in perfect detail, but as if he were looking at an image of the truck from the edge of a photograph.

At the same moment, he began to closely listen to what was being said in the cage. They were talking about the object actually projecting the image of itself. That made sense with at he was seeing on the screen.

"Thank you, Sid. Can you send me a copy of these?" William asked.

Sid typed for a few seconds.

"It's in your email." Sid said.

"Good. Please get those other pictures."

William walked out of the room. He began to feel like this quest to get concrete evidence of covert operations was finally coming together. He thought he might finally finish what his father had stared.

Chapter 25

Tommy was always just a little nervous crossing the Bethel Bridge. It was an old rusty beast, built in 1890. It was the last of the old bridges left on the river. It had been made a historical landmark a few years before. A small group was trying to raise funds to restore it. It was three spans of iron that hung ten feet above the river. It was only wide enough for one car at a time. At the time it was built, it was the only bridge for twenty miles in either direction. Before the bridge had been built, most of the traffic across the river had gone across a ford made of logs and stones at the same place on the river.

Many of the stones that had been part of the ford had been used in the original pilings at the ends of the bridge. The pilings on the north side of the river had been washed out in the flood of 1980. They had been replaced by concrete. Other than that, the bridge was essentially the same as when it had been built.

Now at night in the lights of the Chevelle, it looked like an eerie skeleton of rust and potholed pavement. It made Tommy think of something in a post-apocalyptic science fiction movie, or something one would see in the bayous of Louisiana right before a zombie attack.

Once across the bridge, Tommy turned east on the River Road. It twisted and wove through the fields, following the curves of the river. The road like the bridge had seen better days, but still served a purpose for reaching many of the large farms and the homes north of the river. They followed the River Road to the Emerald Bridge and recrossed the river. This put Tommy and Michelle about a mile from where Tommy anticipated the perimeter around the quarry would be set up.

They could see the smokestack at Shawnee as soon as they cleared the tall trees that hung over the road and bridge. The road they were on led almost directly toward it. The majority of the sodium arc lights that usually shined up the side of the stack had been turned off. This caused the stack to be oddly silhouetted against the glow from the moon. The only light on the smokestack was the flashing red beacon at the top, meant to warn off low flying aircraft. Tommy thought it was for show only. He was sure the air space over and around the pit had already been restricted. It would only take a couple minutes for a jet, scrambled from the nearby air national guard base, to reach the quarry.

Tommy and Michelle stopped at the corner, a mile from the perimeter.

"What is the plan?" Michelle asked.

"I think play the local yokel and drive straight toward it, 'til we hit the perimeter. This car has plates from Emerald County, so we can pretend to be looky loos. Once we are turned away, we can start looping around," Tommy said.

"Okay. That sounds good. What if they decide to arrest us?"

"They won't. I'm guessing the perimeter will be MPs, even if the people in charge aren't military. The last thing they want is to get saddled with civilians. It is just too messy. We will have to be careful after the first contact, but we won't have any problems at the first place we encounter. We just can't make a nuisance of ourselves."

"I hope you're right," Michelle said.

"This should take us to the Canal Road. I'm guessing there will be a road block just the other side of it. If there is, then we're lucky. I think, if they are south of the Canal Road, we can sneak in." Tommy said.

"Sneak in?" Michelle asked incredulously.

"I think so, but let's wait to see where the perimeter is. It may be a moot point."

He pulled through the stop sign and headed toward the smokestack. Soon they saw the lights of huge military vehicles. They were pale in comparison to the glow from a portable flood light, with its own self-contained generator.

As they got close to the barricade, one of the vehicles turned on flashing lights. One of the MPs strolled forward.

Tommy pulled up slowly and rolled down the window. The MP walked up.

"I'm sorry, sir, this is a restricted area," he said.

"I know. I got a cousin who lives just down the road," Tommy said and pointed to his right down Canal Road. "He is wantin' some help getting some stuff together to get out of here for a while. Can I go that way?"

"Yeah, that shouldn't be a problem. The perimeter of the restricted area runs just south of this road, then turns south at Road 73, that way." The MP pointed west. "And Road 117, that way." He pointed east.

"Okay. That's no problem. By the way, what unit are you guys with? I spent two years with the 109th back during Desert Storm." Tommy said.

"We're with the 53rd. We do most of the security for the engineers."

Tommy noticed there was no insignia on the man's uniform.

"Nice. Well thanks a lot. I hope it stays quiet out here for you," Tommy said.

He rolled up the window, put on his turn signal and headed west.

"That went well. And I think we can get in," Tommy said.

"How?" Michelle asked.

"I'll show you in a couple minutes," Tommy said.

They drove west on the Canal Road.

Chapter 26

"Now what?" Hedwick asked.

"Pull it back about a yard and see what happens." Robert said.

Sue grabbed the controls of the winch. Slowly the cable wound back onto the spool. When BARRy had been pulled back about a foot, the monitors all blinked back to life as the robot began to wake back up.

"That's interesting." Sue said. "It is absorbing all the energy that comes into range."

She waited for the robot's control computer to reboot. After about twenty seconds, the control prompt appeared on the screen directly in front of her. She typed a few key strokes and waited. She watched the infrared and visual monitors.

After another twenty, seconds she gave a long "Hmm. I think I understand what is going on. Look here," she said and pointed at the infrared monitor. "See the beam. That is just a simple laser pointer. The beam stops here, or at least appears to, but on the visual there is a faint red spot where the beam would hit the object."

She tapped in a few more keystrokes. The beam of the laser pointer angled down toward the ground. As the beam moved across the surface of the object, the red dot on the object moved. When the beam moved off the surface. The dot disappeared. It should have been visible on the surface of a large rock in front of the object.

"Good. Very interesting. I believe the object is absorbing the beam. It is then compensating the visual image that it is projecting. The compensation only is active for the image of the object. As I hope you noticed, once the beam moved off the object, the false image of the laser spot disappeared. That leaves us with a possible mechanism. First, the object is absorbing all radiation inside the perimeter, which is just in front of BARRy. Second, it is generating visual images of itself, which are actually being compensated, and transmitting images of the surroundings which are static.

"So that is why the laser didn't appear on the rocks?" Hedwick asked.

"I believe so. Let me try something," Sue said

She flipped two switches. The lights that had been set up to keep the object lit, went out. After a few seconds, she flipped the switches back on and the lights came back on. Sue looked at the visual image monitor. She backed up the recording. After a few minutes examining a sequence of four frames very closely, she smiled.

"That makes more sense. There is about a fifty millisecond delay between the object image appearing and the surrounding area appearing. Imagine the surrounding area is 3D modeled and lighting can be accounted for, but new information like a laser is outside the model's parameters. At least that is a working theory," she said.

"So, how does that affect how we approach the object?" Robert asked.

"The real question is whether anything living can approach that thing. Would the absorption of the electromagnetic energy even apply to the small electric impulses that run a living organism?" Sue said.

"That would explain what happened to those workers, but they died outside of where the absorption perimeter is. And it wouldn't account for why they looked like they were boiled from the inside out," Hedwick said.

Robert grimaced. His brow furrowed. There was a heavy silence for about fifteen seconds.

He said what they were all thinking. "We'll have to put something alive inside the perimeter and see what happens."

Sue stood and walked to the back of the cage. She opened a double shielded cabinet and pulled out a small cage. Inside was a hairless rat.

"I was afraid we might need a test subject after I saw what had happened to those men," Sue said.

"How do we get it inside the blackout area?" asked Hedwick.

"We can attach a little something I've been working on to BARRy. It is a boom arm that shouldn't be affected. All the electrical parts are in the end closest to BARRy's chassis. The end that would go inside doesn't have any electrical parts. It is only mechanical with physical linkages. We can extend the boom fully with 'Slick' here at the end and see what happens when we move BARRy right up to the perimeter." Sue said.

"OK. That sounds like a plan. Bring BARRy back," said Robert.

Chapter 27

A half mile down the road from the checkpoint, there was a dip in the road. It was not much, but it was enough to hide the taillights of the Chevelle from the MP's at the checkpoint. The dip was due to an old canal access trail that was cut down to the level of the canal. It was here that Tommy slowed the car to a crawl.

"Over there, just under the willow, do you see the darker shadow?" Tommy asked.

"Yes. What is it?" Michelle asked.

"There's a drainage ditch and a tunnel that comes up from the pond at the bottom of the pit. They dug it about 35 years ago to run drainage lines to take care of overflow water. I found out about it when I spent a couple summers working there in high school. And, I don't think it has been used in a long time. The drainage ditch runs in about seventy-five feet from the tree and then drops into the tunnel." Tommy said.

"How do you plan on getting in there?" Michelle asked.

"I don't think it will be on the maps. The county topographic maps are forty years old. Do you remember that whole issue Alex Groves had because of those maps?" Tommy said.

"Oh yeah. I'd forgotten about that. He built a pond and the area around it was dry, but the maps still showed the area as creek bottom. He wasn't able to get a permit to build a house or something. So, do we go in right away or do we wait?"

"I think we need to finish our rounds. Then make a decision," Tommy answered. "And I'm thinking of a new plan. I think there is enough cover from my house to that ditch. I might be able to get there, if I can get to my house first."

They sped up and drove for a couple minutes, slowing down as they passed the roadblocks at County Road 87 and Road 83. When they reached CR 73, there was no military presence. It was dark. From the intersection, the factory portion of Shawnee showed in profile against the rising moon. The big conveyors that rose forty feet up into the sky and carried different size gravel to giant piles looked like a giant, mechanical, spider.

Tommy turned off the car lights. He pulled into a farmer's lane facing directly toward Shawnee. He dug under the seat, and pulled out an ancient pair of binoculars. Slowly he scanned the horizon. He paused, put the binoculars down and sighed.

"I think the outer perimeter is slack, but the inner perimeter is stiffer. Look at the gantry just south of the stack. There is a gun nest. I can see at least two men with weapons," Tommy said.

Michelle looked through the binoculars. "I don't see... Wait there. Oh crap. Where is that compared to where that tunnel is?"

"It is about 300 yards from there. I don't think there is a good line of sight to the tunnel opening from…"

Suddenly a vehicle turned onto the road headed toward them.

"Shoot!" Tommy said. "Uhh. Take off your shirt"

"What?" Michelle said.

"If it's the MPs we need to convince them we're just parking." Tommy said.

Michelle understood, and started unbuttoning her shirt. Tommy stuffed the binoculars under the seat. Michelle pulled off her shirt, and Tommy undid his belt and the zipper on his pants. As nervous as he was, he could not help but notice the lacy bra Michelle was wearing.

The vehicle was indeed a group of MPs. They shined a big spotlight on the car. The big Hummer parked directly behind the Chevelle. A tall muscular, mustached man got out of the passenger side. He walked around to the driver's side of the car. He had a big flashlight in one hand, although the spotlight shining on the car made it unnecessary. His other hand was on the butt of his sidearm. He let the beam of his flashlight linger on Michelle as she held her shirt up against her chest and blushed.

Tommy looked up with a sheepish grin. "Is there a problem?" He asked then he winked at the MP.

"No, sir. We're just on patrol, and wanted to be sure everything was alright. How are you this evening, ma'am." The MP said. He continued to ogle Michelle.

"I'm fine." Michelle said. She did not look at the MP.

"Alright folks, sorry to bother you. Have a good evening." The MP said. He winked at Tommy. He went back to the Hummer.

Tommy could see him telling the driver about them with a smile on his face. The Hummer drove away.

Tommy waited a minute, then followed slowly, with his lights off.

"That was too close." He said.

"I'm always astounded by the power of boobs." Michelle said. Then she smiled at Tommy as she buttoned the top button on her shirt.

Chapter 28

"Ok Slick. Lets hope this works, or it could be messy," Sue said to the rat. She looped a piece of bungee cord under the cage, and around the end of the boom arm. She looked through the slit in the shield and saw BARRy rounding the corner of the limestone wall, back into sight. A few minutes before she had given the return command that caused BARRy to reverse its course and return to the point of origin. She began to work on the other end of the boom, loosening the bolts that would attach it to the robot. BARRy rolled up like an obedient dog.

"Robert, could you help me with this? It is a little too heavy for me to handle, with the counterweight and all," Sue said.

"Of course." Robert grabbed the end that Sue had just been working on. He agreed that it was likely more than she would have been able to lift easily. On the other hand, he had seen her throw forty pound bags of sand nearly twenty feet during a rescue mission. Sue guided the bar to a heavy bracket on the side of the robot. She inserted two bolts and loosely thumbed the nuts.

"That will do. Just give me a minute to tighten this up. Then we can send BARRy back around the corner." She reached into a pocket of her light blue overalls and pulled out a small power drill with a socket on it and a box end wrench. She tightened the nuts.

"There we go. Let's see what this thing does to a living organism. I just hope we don't end up with rat pudding," Sue said.

Sue reseated herself in front of the monitors. She typed in a new command line. BARRy rolled toward the corner of the rock wall again.

The comment about rat pudding stirred Robert's memory. He thought of his freshman year in college. He had gone to a Halloween party at "Kensington Place," a giant, sprawling, Victorian wreck of a house located a couple blocks from campus. Robert's friends, Jimmy and Elliot, lived there along with a half dozen other students. Jimmy's parents had bought the house when his older brother went to school. They had more than covered the loan payments and utilities with the rent they got from the other students who lived there.

Robert had loved "Kensington place". There was an immense parlor to the side as one entered the front door. On the other side of the entry was a massive library. All those who lived there pooled their books and studied at one of the three huge library tables that dominated one end of the room. On the other end of the room were four long, hefty sofas bought from the local consignment shop, arranged in a large square. Two large coffee tables were set side by side in the middle of the square. Books and magazines related to the residents' majors were stacked there for any visitor to peruse. This had been Robert's favorite place in the house. For atmosphere, during most of the year there was a fire in the fireplace. A small wet bar, with drinks and snacks was on the wall by the rear door. A coffee pot was almost always just starting or just finishing a new pot of coffee. An empty coffee can sat on the wet bar with a handwritten note saying simply "thanks" taped to it.

Robert spent countless hours there, first as a guest, then living in one of the rooms on the second floor. He had initially been amazed that the front door was always unlocked. But he never came or went when there was not at least one other person in the house. After he moved in he understood that, somehow or other, it was only friends who ever came there.

It was an ideal house for a Halloween party. The house was very much reminiscent of the Addams Family mansion at all times of the year. For Halloween, Elliot had taken great pains in making sure there were dim lights and cobwebs and dust everywhere to amplify the effect.

The party was the first time Robert had gotten drunk. He had gotten buzzed before, but not drunk; especially not drunk like this. He began by having a big cup full of the witches' brew—the punch for the party. He was not aware at the time, and only found out later, that the punch had been spiked with a fifth of vodka and a fifth of tequila.

After the witches brew, he felt relaxed. His judgment was slightly impaired. This impairment led him to playing a game of euchre in which the team losing each hand had to take a drink. He had a run of bad cards. By the end of the third game, he and his partner had killed a off a bottle of rum.

Robert had found a chair in the corner of the parlor, and was trying to sober up. Elliot, who was carrying a gallon jug of cheap red wine, came up to him. Elliot had told Robert it was a tradition at "Kensington Place" to drink a toast with the host, whenever one came to a party. By this point Robert's judgment was very fuzzy. He did not want to seem an ungrateful guest, so he drank a glass of wine.

Shortly after drinking the wine, he managed to remember he had a midterm the next day. He felt that he really must go back to the dorm to rest. He got a ride back to the dorm with the designated driver, Angel Tracy.

By the time he had reached the dorm, he had forgotten again about the exam and noticed his neighbor's door was open. He stood leaning against the door jam, watching "The Wizard of Oz" on the TV while Pink Floyd's "Dark Side of the Moon" played through the speakers of an elaborate stereo system.

There were several people in the room, all of them drunk or on the way to being drunk. Robert had learned that the business school had no classes on Fridays. This was Thursday night. All of the students in the room were business majors. He was invited in and offered some beer. They also offered him some of what they called rat pudding.

Rat pudding was a mixture of crushed Oreos and cherry pie filling. On the surface it sounded good, but it clashed horribly with all the alcohol Robert had drank. The results were tragic. About five minutes after he had finished his serving of the sweet stuff he felt terribly nauseated. He excused himself and went to throw up.

He made it to the exam the next day, but had paid dearly. He was hung over in epic proportions. After the exam he went back to his room, drank a half gallon of water and slept through 'til Saturday morning.

"Reaching the corner now..." Sue said.

Robert snapped back to the present. He was slightly concerned about all of the daydreams he had been having lately. The psych doctor had said that it was a coping mechanism due to lack of sleep. That certainly applied.

He looked through the slit in the shielding. He watched BARRy round the corner and gazed at the various monitors. One of the screens displayed the rat cage at the end of the boom arm. The rat was curled up in a ball in the corner of the cage, quivering. Robert felt bad for the animal, but there was no way he would send one of his people close to that thing until he knew they would be safe.

The minutes dragged as BARRY slowly rolled to the perimeter where the robot had previously stopped responding. Sue halted the robot just shy of where the boom would enter the perimeter. The rat was now running back and forth in the cage.

"I think I'll put the rat in for five minutes, and bring him back out. That should give us an idea of what will happen," Sue said.

"Alright. Let's hope for no rat pudding," Robert said.

BARRy rolled forward ten more feet. As it did Robert, Hedwick and Sue all held their breath. The cage, the rat and the end of the boom disappeared.

Chapter 29

William listened to the conversation that the three in the cage were having. He wanted to see what was happening as well as listen. He walked back to the office where he had left his computer. He reached under the edge of the door and turned off the sensor and walked in. The room was only lit by the light of the monitor and the firefly glow from the USB thumb drive.

The light reminded him of the glow of the instrument panel on his father's old Plymouth Fury. He thought about how he and his father had spent almost a week driving from Philadelphia to Los Angeles. His father had worked for a company that supplied paint additives to the motion picture industry. It was not glamorous work, but it allowed William and his father to travel to California about once a year. They usually made a two week vacation out of it. This particular trip occurred during a slump in the company's business, so William's father had been able to take off more time than usual. William had just gotten his learner's permit. His father had thought it would be a great opportunity for him to get some excellent driving practice.

It had been summer and they had driven mostly at night. The car had no air conditioning and the heat during the day was just too intense inside the black vinyl guts of the beast. He could remember being allowed to drive in the remote, almost unpopulated stretches in West Texas. He had been amazed there were long miles along those roads where there were no lights to be seen and no other cars for an hour at a time. It had seemed to him, on those long nights under the moon, that the car really was a two ton beast and the engine was the heart, beating, thrumming wildly as the miles rolled away in the dark.

Growing up in the suburbs of an eastern city, he did not realize what a truly giant country the United States was. He had been to California before this road trip. But he had flown. During the late night drives, he realized there was no way to get a feel for the vastness of the country when you are flying over it.

During the trip they had talked much more than they did when they flew. The long hours, the lack of landscape and frequent loss of radio stations gave them time to talk. William remembered one conversation in particular. He could trace his being in this very place, watching and gathering evidence, directly to that conversation.

"Bilbo, I think it is time I told you a few things that I have learned over the years. These are things that you won't learn in school. Some of it is dangerous information. Do you think you can handle it?" Williams's father had asked.

William had thought it was going to be about women or his mother's death when he was three or some great wisdom that only the venerable old age of forty-two could bestow. He nodded.

"There are things that go on in the world that are done in the shadows. There are people who work for the government, who would just as soon you didn't know they exist. A lot of information about many things is hidden from the citizens of the United States. The government will say these people don't exist, but I believe they do. I believe there have been things that would really shake up the world if they got out, that have been covered up by people in the government. When I was in Vietnam, I saw some things that I had no explanation for. There were people who were dressed up like Army, who told us that what we saw wasn't real. They gave us explanations that didn't make any sense. I believe I saw a spacecraft. They told me it was a weather balloon. A balloon couldn't move the way that thing moved. I was told to forget it. But I never have been able to."

"Did you see an alien?" William asked.

"I didn't see any creatures or anything like that. But the thing I saw, I think it was a spaceship. No matter what they told me I know it wasn't something from earth. There have been too many other things as well. I tried to get a copy of the reports about it when I was discharged. All I got was a couple pages that had most of the writing blacked out. Why would they do that, if there wasn't something they want to hide? I've tried to get other information since then. Every time it is the same thing, most of the stuff is blacked out. I believe there are a lot of things that the government knows that the people haven't been told."

William looked at his father, wide eyed. He did not know what to say. Initially he had thought it was a joke. His father had a wicked sense of humor and liked to tell elaborate stories as set ups for his jokes. Somehow there was something so earnest in his father's face that William knew this was not a joke. From that moment, William had begun to think about the things his father told him. He had decided then that he would help his father to expose these things to the world.

Since then, William had learned much about what had gone on in that shadow world his father had talked about. William had dug up the original reports about what his father had seen in Vietnam. He was convinced it was one of the objects secretly described as "likely extraterrestrial." He had learned also the usefulness of redaction in controlling information. The psychological distance, from that late night drive so many years ago to being on the point of getting the evidence he needed to expose everything, seemed light years distant. William felt he was on the brink of accomplishing what had started in the heat of the West Texas night.

William sat at the desk and looked at the monitor. He hit the F11 key. The screen split into four sections. One was the view of the little camera he had planted. The other three were cloned images of what was on three of the monitors in the cage. The one he was most interested in was the one that showed the view from the robot's perspective. There in the foreground was the boom arm to which was attached a cage with a rat inside. He was amused by the cliché of using a lab rat for the experiment.

William watched as the rat became more and more agitated. As the countdown in his earpiece ended, the rat disappeared. His breath caught. He was stunned. He had not understood the full meaning of the discussion about projected images until now. He pulled up another small window on the computer and double checked that the last few seconds of video had been recorded. He knew he had what he needed. Now he watched, entranced, to see what would happen when the cage came back.

Chapter 30

Tommy and Michelle drove slowly to the southern edge of the evacuation area. Neither spoke. Michelle was too embarrassed. Tommy was lost in his memories. He was thinking about the last time he had seen his wife in a negligee.

"So. What way do we go?" Michelle broke the silence.

"Left here, east. Then I think we can go back north on 137. There are mostly beans in the fields along there so we should be able to get a good view," Tommy answered.

They drove on, watching to the north as they went. At the next crossroad there was another vehicle with four MPs. Tommy waved briefly as he went by. They could see nothing, other than the military presence at the crossroads, that was any different than the usual view of the quarry. Tommy was very familiar with the view. This was his usual route home from work.

They tuned north on 137. The view was very much the same. Tommy repeated the maneuver of pulling into a farmer's lane to face directly toward the quarry.

"Do you want me to take off my shirt again?" Michelle said.

Tommy laughed. "Not right now. Just keep an eye out for anyone turning onto the road. I don't want to get surprised again."

He pulled the binoculars back out from under the seat and scanned the horizon. After thirty seconds he sighed and put the binoculars down.

"There are two more gun nests on this side of the quarry, just like those on the other side."

"So we don't try to sneak in that way either. I'm becoming more concerned that the tunnel you told me about is going to be the best route," Michelle said.

"I think so," Tommy said.

He pulled the car back onto the road. They continued driving north. Tommy, no longer looking at the factory, was driving faster. His mind was made up.

"I think I'll wait 'til tomorrow and go to my house, or rather you will go. I'll be hiding in the trunk. I'll stay at the house after you leave." Tommy said.

"Then what?"

"I think I can get from my house to the canal without being seen. From there I think I can get to that tunnel. I just hope they haven't found it."

"What will you do when you get to the end of the tunnel? What makes you think they won't just shoot you if they catch you?" Michelle asked.

Tommy could hear the beginning of panic in her voice. "I don't know. Maybe they would. I'm just wanting to get a close enough to see that thing for myself. That's all. If I can see it. If I can be sure, then I have a good idea of what to do next. I have to see it though," Tommy said.

"It won't do you any good to see it if you are dead," Michelle said.

"I know. Don't worry. I'll give you a chance to talk me out of it tomorrow. And maybe I'll think better of it by the light of morning," Tommy said.

"Alright. I'll accept that. I really could use some sleep myself. How about you?" Michelle asked.

"Yeah, I could. There is just one more thing I think we should do first. We need to go to the grocery store," Tommy said.

Tommy performed a three point turn and headed back toward town. He had seen enough. He did not expect to learn anything new by completing the full circle of the quarry. He really could use something else to eat and some bottles of water for the next couple days.

Michelle was looking toward the quarry and saw, or thought she saw, in the distance a flash of blue light over the quarry. It was only a flash and she could not be sure of it.

"Did you see that?" Tommy asked.

"I saw something. Like a flash over the quarry. Are they blasting or something?" Michelle asked.

"No. Not blasting. When there is a blast there is a big cloud of dust. I don't see any dust. And there isn't a flash either. I don't know what that was," Tommy said.

"I want to go in with you. I want to see that thing too." Michelle said.

"Hmm. If I say no, will it stop you?"

"No," Michelle said.

"Then we need to come up with a new plan," Tommy said.

"What kind of beer do you like? I'm buying at the store," Michelle said.

"I'll drink anything. Beer sounds like a good idea. I could drink a couple myself."

Chapter 31

"Where did the rat go?" Robert asked. He was trying to keep calm, but both Sue and Hedwick could pick up the heightened level of stress in his voice.

"Not to worry," Sue said. "It just confirms in another way what I said about the object absorbing all the frequencies and projecting a manufactured visual image. Once the rat passed in, it became overwhelmed by the transmitted image. Not entirely unexpected, but still stunning to see."

Hedwick felt the ground start to vibrate. At first she was not sure. It felt almost like her feet were tingling from standing in one place too long. Then it began to be a more intense sensation.

"What is that?" Hedwick asked.

"I don't know. The motion detectors are showing an 800 hertz vibration that is growing in amplitude," Sue said.

There was sudden flash of blue-white light. It was faint but distinct. All of the monitors blinked off and back on. The vibration stopped.

"What was that?" Robert asked.

"I don't know that either. It is going to take me a minute to check a few things," Sue said.

"Did that mess up any of the equipment?" Robert asked.

"Not any here. But BARRy is resetting. How is your backside? I think we just got probed. Think radar or sonar but at a different set of frequencies," Sue said.

Sue and Hedwick had the idea at the same time. They looked at each other. "Sonar," they said in unison.

""What about sonar?" Robert asked.

"The thing appears to absorb all kinds of electromagnetic energy. But, sonar works on sound waves which are physical disturbance of the medium through which it travels, a vibration, not electrical. We may be able to use that to get a first hand view of the object. I don't have any sonar equipment but I do have an idea," Sue said.

"What do you need to set up a sonar imaging of that thing?" Hedwick asked.

"A fish finder should do the job," Sue said.

"There is a Wally World about thirty minutes from here. I remember passing it on the way in. They would have one. Send a message to Billings and have him go pick one up," Robert said.

"Sounds like a plan. I don't really like the idea of that thing—or more specifically, what ever is responsible for that thing—only allowing us to see what it wants us to see." Hedwick said.

Sue shook her head. "That is a common element of much science fiction. Humans believe that aliens would want to disguise themselves. It is the whole 'you can't handle the truth' lie. I seriously doubt that real aliens would give a rat's ass about what we think. Any species that is advanced enough to get here would be more than advanced enough to defend themselves against any weapon we could throw at them, short of nukes. A far more likely scenario is that the absorption of all the electromagnetic energy is one of the ways the object gathers energy from the environment. It is like using solar energy on a much broader range of the EM spectrum, and very efficient. And the fact that they are transmitting in visual light, I think, is a courtesy and not a disguise. A much better disguise would be to absorb all of it and not put out an image or put out an image that doesn't show the object. But I think we will find out more with a little sonar."

"I suppose you are right," Hedwick assented. "But why here? Why is there anything here to trigger the conversation in the first place? I can't help but wonder why, if the image being transmitted is accurate, is the object buried in the rock? Why isn't it just hovering or not landed on the White House lawn?"

"We won't know that until we can find out more about the 'what' of this thing. Only then will the other pieces begin to fall in place," Sue said.

In their discussion about the sonar they had totally forgotten about the rat.

"What about the rat?" Robert asked.

Sue typed in several keystrokes. She hit enter. BARRy rolled slowly backward. The cage appeared. The rat was gone. There was no fur, no blood, no evidence of the rat whatsoever other than the cage.

"Hmm. That's interesting," Sue said.

"Interesting?" Robert shouted. "What happened to the rat?"

"I don't know. But I think we have our answer about whether we can go in there." Sue said.

"Now what do we do?" Robert asked.

"We use the sonar to see if we can 'see' that thing that way. And I think I'd like to see if I can get a sample of the air and earth inside there. Beyond that I need to think. And I need to sleep. I'm going to bring BARRy back here then to take a nap until the fish finder gets here," Sue said.

Sue typed in the return code for BARRy, stood up and walked out of the cage. Robert and Hedwick looked at each other. Robert smiled and shook his head. Hedwick was incredulous. Wordlessly they followed her back toward the main office building, back up out of the pit.

Chapter 32

Tommy and Michelle walked into the Grove Hill grocery store, the sort of place that can only be found in small towns, in very rural areas far from the nearest supercenter all-in-one mega store. The only thing that kept the Grove in business was the convenience factor. It was at least twenty miles to the nearest "real" grocery. The locals just found it easier when they needed a dozen eggs, a loaf of bread or the fixings to cure a late night nacho craving to go here. The prices were a little higher. After gas went over two dollars a gallon, the difference in price was generally offset by the savings in the cost of gas required to drive to anywhere else.

The other thing Grove Hill had going for it, was that it was owned by local folks. The Sitclers had been around for at least six generations. They had always run the grocery. Back in the original days of the town, there was the Sitcler General Store, the Sitcler Livery and the Sitcler Hotel. Before that the Sitclers had run the trading post on the river where goods came up the canal to the lake. History and "trading with the locals" still counted for a lot here. To many of the locals, going to one of the "big boxes" felt almost like betraying their own history. Some even felt a little guilty when they went out of town to shop, even if they were going there because the local stores did not have what they needed.

Michelle grabbed a cart, and headed slowly through the store. She and Tommy were discussing what snacks they wanted when, rounding a corner at the end of an aisle, they ran into Michelle's boss.

"Michelle! Where have you been?" Sam Keep said.

Sam was a tall, thin man whose bald head shone in the fluorescent lights of the store. He had a tendency to wear blue jeans and denim shirts most of the time. Michelle kept count and was able to pick out four pairs of jeans and eight different shirts. The basic look rarely changed, with the exception of the shoes he wore. For casual wear, he wore a pair of red Chuck Taylor high tops. For summer it was Birkenstock sandals. For winter, a pair of ancient leather hiking boots. For formal occasions he wore his polished, black chucka boots with the silver zippers on the inside of the ankles.

Michelle was momentarily stunned, but recovered quickly. "Oh didn't you get my message? I'm following Tommy around. His house is inside the evacuation zone. I'm doing a story of what this whole thing is like from the perspective of an evacuee. You can get the factual stories from any of the major outlets, probably better than what I can do. This is a more local story." Michelle said.

"I didn't get the message. But then I haven't been in the office all day." Sam said.

"I talked to Hillary, so you might not have gotten it anyway." Michelle said.

Sam gave a grunt and a smile. "True."

Hillary Piretti was notorious for losing copy and forgetting to give messages. The only way she kept her job was nepotism. She was the twenty-five-year-old widow of Sam's nephew. Joe had been the only relative Sam had after his brother had died of cancer. Joe and Hillary had been married three weeks before Joe had been deployed to Afghanistan. He had never come back. Sam felt that, by extension, Hillary was his only family. No matter how ditzy she was, she had a good heart and Sam felt she deserved to have a little protection.

"I see the idea as maybe a four part series: initial reactions, the trip to the house, what comes next, then maybe a follow-up story in a couple weeks." Michelle said.

"Sounds good. When do I get the first story?" Sam said.

"Day after tomorrow. I'm going to the house with Tommy tomorrow, and I'll get you both stories after that. I figure you can run them Thursday and Friday with a teaser for the third one to print maybe Tuesday." Michelle said.

"That's fine. Keep me posted. And stop leaving messages with Hillary," Sam said. He winked at Michelle, chuckled a little and walked toward the register.

Michelle looked at Tommy. "Sorry," She said

"I'm just glad you recovered that quickly. That could have been a disaster," Tommy said.

"Sam has teased me about having a crush on you ever since I did those other stories. So I don't think it took too much to sell him,"

Michelle said.

"Either way, I'm glad."

Tommy and Michelle reached the deli counter. Tommy grabbed a couple of the pre-made subs from the case and a pound container of potato salad. This was a meal he ate a couple times a week. The grocery was on his way home from work and often he didn't feel like cooking. Sometimes he would grab this on his way in to work to eat for his meal break. Michelle raised an eyebrow and grabbed a bag of fresh vegetables from the cold case opposite the deli counter.

Tommy was shocked. Michelle at that moment reminded him of his wife so much that he was momentarily stunned. The look and the grabbing of the vegetables was exactly something she would have done. It took his breath away. He grabbed hard onto the handle of the cart. Michelle saw and suspected the reason. She pretended not to notice. She knew he was able to compartmentalize his grief most of the time. She also knew that grief could be triggered by the strangest things.

"Okay, water and beer," Tommy said.

He had regained himself quickly, moving the cart across the back aisle of the store. Michelle followed. She was attracted to Tommy. She let herself admit it, but knew there would always be someone else in the room. That was the thing that had kept her from trying to be more than a friend. Perhaps, if they got through the next few days, she might reconsider her position. For now, she knew she could not think about it.

Tommy picked up a case of water and a case of beer and plunked them down in the cart.

"Is there anything else you want?" Tommy asked.

"Maybe a bag of pretzels," Michelle said and grabbed some off the shelf. "That should do it."

The walked to the register and put their purchases on the ancient, tattered conveyor belt.

"Evening, Tommy." The cashier said. She was the daughter of one of Tommy's cousins. Tommy had not been paying attention and was momentarily surprised.

"Oh. Hi, Jess. Sorry. My mind was wandering. How's your dad?" Tommy asked.

"He's good. He's up at Indian River this week. He claims he is fishing, but I know he just goes up there and sits in the boat listening to the radio and drinking beer. But he works hard. He deserves it. Are you having a party or something?" Jessica asked.

"No. Just getting a few things for the cabin. I got evacuated as part of the mess at the quarry. So I'm going to stay out there for awhile," Tommy said. He passed Jessica two twenty dollar bills. "Thanks Jess. See you later."

As Michelle and Tommy walked to the Chevelle, there was a flash of lightning in the southwest. A wind had begun to blow. There was a scent on the wind. The smell was a combination of ozone and the deep, earthy, fungal smell of freshly tilled earth. The air was cooler than it had been when they had gone into the store. A storm was coming.

Chapter 33

Hedwick and Robert came out onto the level between the pit and the office. Sue was almost to the building.

Robert thought, "She moves so fast for someone so small."

"How do we deal with not being able to get to this thing?" Hedwick asked.

"We may have to end up burying it. This place and the cover story would be conducive to that. It would be a lot worse if this was in a big city," Robert said.

"True. Would the thing would allow itself to be buried?" Hedwick asked.

"I'm not sure. This is, of course, the last option. I'm not ready to entertain that 'til we hear what Sue says. I've sometimes wondered how her brain works, then realized that knowing would probably make my head explode," Robert said.

"Yeah. I think she understands the world on a whole different level from most of the rest of us," Hedwick said.

They were silent as they crossed the rest of the way to the office building. The crunch of the gravel underfoot, this time, impacted by the mystery of what happened to the rat, reminded him of the grinding sound his ankle had made when he had broke it. He had, years ago, been on vacation. He was sixteen and fearless. He had just started driving. On a late summer evening he was driving a car full of teens. They stayed at the same cluster of vacation cabins and he was bringing them back from the movie theater in the neighboring town.

He was in his grandmother's gigantic Thunderbird, speeding along a winding road that ran beside the shore of the lake. The driver of the car that hit them was drunk. All his passengers were hurt, but none badly. The only thing Robert remembered was the crunch and the lightning flash of pain, as both of the bones in his lower leg snapped, just above the ankle.

Hedwick and Robert reached the office building. As they went through the door, the bright lights forced them to squint. The chill of the air conditioning set goose bumps on their skin.

"Call me when the equipment gets here to make the sonar. I think I'll try to get a little bit of rest," Robert said.

"Okay. And I'll see if the tech guys have had any luck with the phone. I have a few calls to make regarding the evacuation. I'll see you in a little bit," Hedwick said.

Robert went to the office. It was not quite as cool as the hallway. Robert's skin relaxed a little. He no longer felt as if his nipples were going to pop off and run away. Robert never could decide which was worse, being too hot or being too cold. He sometimes felt as if his life revolved around being at one temperature extreme or the other.

He lay down on the couch in the office, and closed his eyes. He had a mental trick he used often to try to sleep. He blamed it partly for his daydreaming, but it was the most effective thing he had found for his frequent bouts of insomnia. He would imagine a place he knew well and try to visualize every detail. By giving complete focus to this task, he was able to put aside what ever else was going on in his head.

He began to imagine Camp Beerman, where he and his grandmother, along with various combinations of cousins, aunts and uncles, vacationed. Camp Beerman was a grouping of small cabins along a slow flowing river that connected two of the small lakes in the northern part of the lower peninsula of Michigan. There were thirteen cabins and a dozen or so private houses that loosely filled the land in the horseshoe shaped bend of the river.

First, Robert pictured the cabin where they usually stayed. It was cabin number thirteen. Despite the unlucky number, it was one of his favorite places growing up. It had a small eat-in kitchen. The fridge was an ancient Westinghouse with a latching door that would trap a child if they got inside. The table was a 1950's chrome and Formica museum piece where his grandmother and he and various other vacationers would play pinochle or euchre late into the night.

The cabin's living room was paneled with knotty pine boards and was dominated by a natural gas heater that hummed and popped when it was running. The furniture was 1960's naughahyde. His grandmother used to joke by saying. "I wonder how many naughas had to die to cover the couch."

Back of the living room down a short hall were the two

bedrooms. They were Spartan, but functional, with only a single chest of drawers and two beds in each room with a nightstand between the beds. The beds had seen better days, but Robert slept well and deeply in them, due to the deep peacefulness he always felt there.

Behind the kitchen, and connected to the living room, was the strangest room in the cabin. It served as a mud room, having a tile floor and the cabin's second outside door. There also was a bed here. His grandmother called it a day bed, but it often was where Robert slept when sufficient relatives were along on vacation to fill the other beds. During the hot summer nights, Robert would have only the screen door between him and the outside. As he lay there in the cool dark with the sound of crickets and bullfrogs in his ears, he slept deeply and dreamlessly. He awoke early to the sounds of the fishermen's boats as they headed up the river to spend the day on the lake.

Behind the row of cabins was an old, wood shed. There was an open area between two ancient weeping willow trees. In the open area was the fire pit where was held, weather allowing, a nightly bonfire starting at twilight and lasting 'til the wee hours of the morning. This was the only place and time in which Robert did not have a curfew. His grandmother knew he was safe and felt it was vacation for him too.

Robert was picturing this bonfire and remembering swinging on the drooping branches of the willows when he fell asleep. He slept deeply. After forty-five minutes, Hedwick came into the room.

She looked at him. She was taken by surprise at how old and tired he looked. The job had aged him faster than he let on. He had not looked like this the last time she had been able to watch him sleep. There were lines around his eyes. He had a deep furrow in his brow that she did not remember. She had last seen him sleep deeply in Arizona. That seemed forever ago, even though it was only a few years. Those few years had aged him twenty. Now Hedwick saw the muscle definition of his jaw had faded. There was the first sign of a sag at the jaw. She watched for another moment, then spoke.

"Robert," she said.

In his half dream, he thought of his grandmother standing on the front stoop of the cabin, calling to him for a meal. He was thinking of one of his favorite meals there: green beans, smoked sausage and little red potatoes all boiled together. The potatoes smashed with a fork on the plate and buttered with salt and pepper were still one of his fondest memories of those vacations.

"Robert," Hedwick said again.

He started, and quickly sat up. He blinked. Much of the age Hedwick had seen on Robert's face faded as the light returned to his eyes and the muscles were no longer slack.

"The equipment is here. Sue is getting it set up. She should be about ready by the time we get back to the cage. There may be a problem. There is a storm coming," Hedwick said.

Robert was fully awake at the word "problem". It was not a word Hedwick used lightly.

"How soon 'til the storm?" Robert asked. He stretched and stood.

Hedwick sat a cup of coffee on the corner of the desk, closest to Robert and then looked at her watch.

"About thirty minutes according to the radar." Hedwick said.

"Then let's get out there and see what we can figure out before it gets here." Robert said. He picked up his coffee and headed out the door.

Chapter 34

Michelle and Tommy got in the car and headed back toward the barn. As they got close, the Chevelle began to rock in the wind. Tommy felt the car pull as the wind strengthened. The lightning flashes became more frequent and brighter in the dark night.

"I hope we make it back to the barn before this storm gets here," Tommy said.

"No kidding!"

They drove on in silence. Tommy was focused on keeping the car on the road. When they were about five miles from the barn, he reached over and turned on the AM radio. It hummed, then the voice of the weatherman cracked over the speakers.

"… heading northeast at thirty miles an hour. Repeating… There is a severe thunderstorm warning for Albert county, Garmin county, Mustic county. There is a tornado watch and severe thunderstorm watch for the entire listening area…"

Tommy flipped off the radio.

"That's going to make things interesting tonight in the barn," Michelle said.

"Oh, it's not too bad. It really is sort of cool in there during a storm. You hear the rain and thunder more clearly than you do from inside a house. The barn has been through a lot of storms, so I feel pretty safe," Tommy said.

"Okay. Will we stay dry?" Michelle asked.

"Sure. The storm is coming from the southwest. And the bunk room is on the east side and it is weather tight. We won't even really feel the wind. It'll be fine."

They pulled into the lane that led to the barn. The rain had not yet started, but they could see it was getting close. Tommy pulled up to the big door.

"Slide over and pull the car in after I open the door," Tommy said.

He got out and shoved open the big door. Michelle slid over

behind the steering wheel and pulled into the dark of the barn. Tommy closed the door behind her. The only light came from the Chevelle's headlights. Michelle turned off the engine and lights. As she did Tommy flipped the switch for the light of the bunk room then came back to the car.

Michelle got out and grabbed the grocery bag. Tommy reached in from the opposite side of the car and got the bottles of water and the beer. Michelle was momentarily distracted by the muscles of his arms as he heaved the forty odd pounds of beverages out of the car.

They went into the bunk room and Tommy shoved the case of bottled water under the bunks and the beer on the floor. Michelle sat the grocery bag on the small table.

As Tommy reached for a beer a giant clap of thunder made them both jump. Tommy laughed and Michelle looked sheepish.

"I told you the thunder was louder in here," Tommy said.

"I see what you mean," Michelle said.

"Beer?"

"Sure," she said.

Tommy twisted the cap off a bottle and handed it to her.

"Tommy. I'm…" Michelle said. Then she hesitated, took a deep pull on the beer, then continued. "Tommy, what do you think that thing is? Don't hedge. Just give me your gut reaction to this."

Tommy was quiet. He looked at the floor for a moment then looked at Michelle. "I can't believe I'm saying this…but, I think it's alien. I've never heard of anything and have never seen anything like that. What else would be so important that someone would kill Gregg?"

Tommy took a drink. He watched Michelle think about what he had just said.

"What do you think it is?" he asked.

"I think you're right," she said.

They stared at each other. The full realization of what they had just said slowly overwhelmed them. Tommy watched Michelle's eyes as they began to show a bit of panic mixed with wonder. He imagined his own expression was much the same.

"Which is why we have to get in there," Tommy finally said. "I'm not one for conspiracy theories, but the way things have been handled so far I have a feeling that thing is going to be permanently covered up. I don't trust what I've seen so far."

"Yeah. And the reasons for covering it up have been written about in dozens of science fiction novels and movies. Take your pick. What is our reason for trying to keep them from covering it up?" Michelle asked.

This stunned Tommy. He had been running on emotions, fear and gut reactions. It was simply something he "knew", without specific logical reasons. A quizzical expression on his face, he gazed at Michelle. His confusion would be funny, if it did not scare him so much.

"I've been thinking, Tommy. I want to be sure that going in there and trying to expose this is really the best idea. I want to be sure that doing that is better than allowing the cover-up. And I want to talk through the consequences of what might happen if we succeed. I'm not saying not to do it. I'm just playing devil's advocate to be sure we are doing the right thing."

Tommy thought for a moment. He had not thought about it that way. "I would know, and I feel I owe it to Gregg. He died for this. And like it or not, we are in the same danger. If I'm going to be in danger, I want to be doing something to deserve it. I don't want to wait for it to come get me. That happened once in my life already. I want to see what is coming."

"I get that. But, will the world be a better place with this knowledge?" Michelle asked.

"Maybe, maybe not. I guess we won't know 'til after the fact. I just prefer to live with the consequences of actions taken, than live with doubts about something not done." Tommy said. He finished his beer in silence. He yawned.

"This is too deep for me when I'm this tired. I need sleep," he said.

"I'm right behind you. As soon as I finish this," Michelle said. "Goodnight."

"Goodnight," Tommy said.

He lay down on the bunk, shoes and all. The ability to fall asleep anywhere in any circumstance served him well again. Soon Michelle heard him breathe deeply and steadily, and she knew he was asleep. She lay on her own bunk after flipping off the light. It took her considerably longer to fall asleep.

Chapter 35

Robert and Hedwick walked out of the office building. To the southwest, they could see lightening flashing high in the folds of a giant thunderhead. The very flat land revealed storms coming long before they arrived. They could hear the distant thunder. To the north was another storm cloud and more lightning. The storm to the north would pass them by. The wind was from the southwest on a direct line from the storm.

"Do you smell that?" Hedwick asked.

Robert took a deep breath. He smelled the mixed aroma of ozone and fungus and the scent that comes after a baked dry field gets rained on after a long dry spell. He recognized the smell. He knew that Hedwick would not know it. She had grown up in the city. The rain on hot dry concrete on a summer day had its own smell. It was different than the smell of rain on the fields.

"It's the smell of rain on the dry ground. Smells different than the city, doesn't it?" Robert said.

"Yes." Hedwick said. "There are darker tones in it. It smells…deeper, older."

"That is the dirt. My grandmother used to say that was the smell of money. But, then she also said that about the smell of manure, so I'm not sure I fully trust her nose," Robert said.

Hedwick smiled. She was thinking she could not decide if she liked or disliked the smell. She had always liked the smell of rain in the city when she was growing up. The smell here was different and it frightened her a little. There was a scent of danger to her. The musky, fungal tones made her think of dark places, scary places. It smelled like something from a tomb.

Then she realized why the smell scared her. It reminded her of being in a cave. She was terrified of caves. The one time she had been in a cave had been on vacation in Tennessee. She had gone into a deep cavern. Initially the slight fear she felt she mistook as excitement. After ten minutes underground she had began to panic.

At one point on the tour, they entered a cavern and the guide turned off the lights. It was the deepest, darkest black she had ever experienced. The panic turned into complete terror. She fought the feeling for about fifteen seconds then began screaming. She had completely lost her mind. She had never gone back into a cave.

She decided she did not like the smell. But the wide open sky above and the wide open spaces around her allayed any fear she felt.

For Robert the smell was the smell of wisdom. The deepness of it reminded him of the times he had spent studying Buddhism in college. His teacher had spoken of the interrelatedness of all things and of the living essence of the earth. She had told Robert how trusting one's senses would allow one to begin to sense that essence.

The summer after he had taken that class he had gone home to the farm. There he made the connection between that smell—the smell of rain on dry earth—and the smell of fresh tilled earth, with things and life older than man, and with wisdom inherent in the earth itself.

Robert breathed deeply again and imagined the earth was telling him that this situation, like all situations would in their own way, work out exactly as they were supposed to. Of course it was his imagination, and he knew it, but he had seen too many things to totally believe the speaking of the earth was impossible.

They followed the same path to the cage they had walked earlier. As they approached they saw Sue was attaching some more equipment to BARRy. She had removed the beam that had carried the rat to its disappearance. The beam had been turned ninety degrees and there was equipment at each end.

Sue saw them approaching. She smiled and waved them over to where she was working.

"Perfect timing. I'm ready to go. With the separation between the two units we should be able to get a resolution of about three inches. I haven't had a chance to test these units to get a good idea of what they can do, but they are designed to work in water so working in air should theoretically improve the resolution. Of course, that is in theory," Sue said.

She flipped a switch on the back of each piece of equipment at the two ends of the beam and headed into the cage. Robert and Hedwick followed.

As before, Sue sat in front of the terminal and typed in the command to send BARRy on its way. It rounded the corner of the limestone outcropping. The object came into view again. This time the robot stopped shy of the perimeter of the dead zone.

Sue typed in some more commands and said, "Watch this monitor. If this works we should have an image appearing here shortly." She hit enter to execute the command to start the improvised sonar.

At first no image appeared. Sue entered another string of commands and an image began to appear. It was fuzzy at first, then began to sharpen and show the image of the object. It was essentially the same as the image that was being projected from the object with the exception of being a direct observation. They were seeing for themselves instead of relying on what they were being shown.

"There it is. Well, at least we aren't being deceived as far as appearances," Robert said.

As they watched the image, a hole in the image began to appear close to where the object penetrated the limestone.

"What's that?" Hedwick asked.

"I'm not sure, but it is in all the images." Sue said.

As they watched the monitors the hole grew to cover nearly half the side of the exposed portion of the object. Then all the monitors went black.

Chapter 36

Tommy quickly fell deeply asleep. He began to have one of the recurrent dreams that presented itself when he was deeply anxious or highly conflicted over a decision he faced in his waking life.

The dream was about an event that had happened the summer between his sophomore and junior years in high school. He was fifteen and had never been kissed. The events as they had really happened involved a girl Tommy had not heard from in fifteen years. In his mind, in his dream, it was his wife who took the place of that girl. Even though Tommy did not meet his wife for two years after the actual event.

As always, the dream began with Tommy marching with a Sousaphone during a parade. He was in the State Fair Band, a conglomeration of 300 high school geeks who formed a marching band was housed at the State Fairgrounds. They performed at many of the events during the fair. Each day at four the band and various other floats and visiting high school bands from around the state would march from one end of the fairgrounds to the other and back in a daily parade.

The weather had been brutal during this summer Tommy dreamed about. The temperature stayed in the high 90's, as did the humidity. The barracks where the band stayed at the fairgrounds, were not air conditioned. The parade had been cancelled on a couple of the hottest days due to the heat being too dangerous for some of the animals in the parade. In his dream, Tommy could feel the heat coming off of the pavement and his sweat soaked shirt clinging to his back.

The dream moved from the parade to Tommy walking hand in hand with his wife through the department of natural resources park at one side of the fairgrounds. It was dark, and during the hour between the last performance of the evening and curfew, when the band members had to be in the barracks. He could feel the warmth of her hand, and the softness of her skin.

They sat on a bench in the shadow between two streetlights. Slowly, Tommy leaned toward her and they kissed. Tommy remembered this kiss and the girl it had really happened with during his waking hours. It was always his wife when he dreamed about it.

After this kiss, his dream shifted to the last night of the fair. It had been another brutally hot day. The band would be leaving after the parade the next day. Tommy and Gina were walking down the midway. They could hear the rumbling of a storm in the distance. The storm approached quickly. It suddenly broke in torrents of rain. Most of the people at the fair ran to get under cover from it. Tommy and Gina just kept walking, enjoying the relief from the heat. As curfew approached Tommy and Gina kissed. In reality it had been the last time Tommy had kissed the girl.

A lightning strike very close to the barn woke Tommy. The dream was fresh in his mind and, when he realized that Gina was not next to him and that he was facing unknown dangers come daylight, he wept. He had gotten good at suppressing the pain of being alone. But every once in a while when he got caught off guard, he would feel overwhelmed and the tears would come.

He listened in the dark. He heard the storm roaring outside. He sat up and reached under the bunk for a bottle of water. The crinkle of the plastic bottle roused Michelle.

"Are you okay?" She asked.

"Yeah. Bad dream," Tommy said.

It was a lie. It was one of the best dreams he had, and he always felt good when he had it. It was waking up that was bad.

"I can't sleep," Michelle said. "Do you want to talk about it?"

"No. Just about my wife. But I don't think I'll be able to go back to sleep for a while. Do you want to take something to help you sleep? I've got some antihistamine."

"Yeah. Hit me. And I think I'll have another beer," Michelle said.

"I think I'll have one too," he said. Tommy gulped about half the bottle of water then he found the diphenhydramine and gave one to Michelle. He popped the top on two more beers and handed one to Michelle.

This time, she popped the pill and chugged the beer. She drained the bottle in three pulls. Tommy was impressed.

"Try and go to sleep. I am going to go walk around in the barn for a while," Tommy said.

"Alright," Michelle said. She lay down and after a few minutes began to doze as the beer and medicine kicked in.

Tommy walked around the barn, slowly nursing his beer. He tried in vain to recapture the feeling of Gina's hand in his and her lips on his.

Chapter 37

"What was that?" Hedwick asked.

"Apparently it doesn't like our play list," Sue said. She looked over her shoulder and smiled at Hedwick. She reached over and hit the switch to start the winch.

"Wait. I want to see if it comes back on. Did you see the hole open in the side of that thing?" Robert said.

Sue flipped off the winch. She opened the cover on one of the shielded cabinets and reached in. A moment later two of the monitors began to show an image of the object, but from a different angle than they had previously shown.

"And here we have plan B," Sue said.

"Excellent! Where are these cameras?" Robert asked.

"One is up on top of that outcropping. The other I one I tapped into from the plant security system. It is about halfway up the smokestack," Sue said.

"So what is that hole?" Hedwick asked.

"I'm guessing it is a physical opening of some sort. Maybe a door or maybe the sound did something to their projection system. If the surface is made up of...," Sue said then stopped short.

A bright light glowed and then flashed in the dark area of the object. It overwhelmed the contrast controls of the cameras for a moment and flared out the screen. Then, as the cameras adjusted, the three in the cage could see what appeared as a square of light amid the utter darkness on the side of the object.

"Is that a door?" Robert asked.

"I don't know," Sue said.

That scared Robert. Those words very rarely passed Sue's lips and, in Robert's experience, they meant trouble.

Sue reached back into the cabinet. Two more monitors came to life. They showed the object from more obtuse angles and from further distances than the other cameras.

"I'm glad I tapped into the quarry's monitoring and surveillance cameras. The quality isn't great, but the equipment is bulletproof. It has to stand up to all the blasting and weather," Sue said.

"So am I," Robert said.

"How many cameras do you have access to?" Hedwick asked.

"Nineteen altogether, but only these four show a direct view of the object. The rest are views of the offices and parking lots and perimeter fences," Sue said.

"Too bad." Hedwick said.

"Hedwick, your eyes are better than mine, are you willing to take a peek around that corner?" Robert asked.

"I thought you would never ask," Hedwick said. She had wanted to get an "eyes on" look at the thing since she saw the first pictures during the initial briefing.

"Sue, have you seen anything that would make it dangerous for Hedwick to go out there?" Robert asked.

"No, the radiation levels are normal—correction, less than normal. There is no evidence of toxins or any other dangers. At least four of the quarry workers were beyond that point when the object appeared and have not experienced any ill effects," Sue said.

"That settles it. Do we have any two-way radios? Is there anything else I need to take out there with me?" Hedwick asked.

"Just yourself. Here is a radio," Sue said. She reached into an overhead bin and pulled out a small black box with a corded headset. "Clip this onto your belt and we can talk like you never left."

Hedwick clipped the box to her belt and put the headset on. She adjusted the microphone and said, "Okay are you reading me?"

"You have to turn it on," Sue said. "Here, now try it."

"Test. Test. Can you read me?" Hedwick said. There was a slight whine of feedback as the microphone picked up her voice and cycled and amplified it.

Hedwick thought about the principal reading the morning announcements over the PA system at her high school. Every morning the announcements would end with just such a squeal.

"Ok, that's good. Turn it off 'til you are outside the cage." Sue said. "Oh, put this on too," Sue took something else from the bin and clipped it onto the headset. She plugged the wire leading from it into the black box on Hedwick's belt. "Now we will see what you see." Sue flipped a switch. A monitor showed the image of what was in front of Hedwick.

"Alright. Go. Take a look around the corner. Then come back. Nothing fancy. Just out and back," Robert said.

Something in his gut told him it would not be that simple. He pushed that feeling away. He had known it often when he had first started this work. Most of the time it was wrong. That feeling was wrong less often now. It was still fallible enough that Robert did not entirely trust it. He just hoped, this time, it was wrong.

Chapter 38

Michelle soon began to doze. After about ten minutes, Tommy could hear her snoring. He listened for awhile, standing just outside the door of the bunk room. He thought of when he used to listen to Gina sleep after waking from nightmares.

At various times in his life he had been plagued by bad dreams. They had started when he was seven. He had fallen out of a tree and broken his left arm and clavicle. The pain medicine he had taken had caused horrific nightmares. After that, the bad dreams came sporadically, sometimes nightly. When he was in high school, his eye doctor suggested he read Freud's "The Interpretation of Dreams."

He had gotten a copy from the library and read it. Then he had read Jung, and then others. None of Tommy's dreams fit how these men interpreted the meanings of dreams. Dreams were supposed to be the subconscious processing the events of life. For Tommy it never made sense. The interpretation did not fit anything in Tommy's life.

For Michelle, dreams had always helped her understand her world and emotions. She had had dreams about tornados when she was feeling overwhelmed by things beyond her control. She had discussed it with her roommate in college. Her roommate had been from Galveston, Texas and dreamed about hurricanes at similar times. The same dream was just transmuted by the location where the individual having the dream grew up: the Midwest had tornados; the south had hurricanes; the west coast, earthquakes. It was the element of nature and its fury that lay in the back of a person's subconscious. It was the 'finger of God'; the agent of chaos that was unpredictable and held incredible destructive power.

And it was one of those tornado dreams Michelle was having. In her dream she was in the Chevelle with a man she did not recognize. The man was not Tommy, but that did not seem to bother Michelle. They were driving toward the storm. Michelle was in the passenger seat, very fearful. The dream shifted and Michelle was behind the wheel. Then she stared into the rearview mirror and the tornado was behind them.

As Michelle drove, the tornado kept pace with the car. Michelle realized then they were driving toward the quarry. Instead of the fields and fences that surround the quarry in reality, Michelle saw that the area around the quarry was paved. Many roads led out from the pit like spokes of a giant wheel. Suddenly the road she was driving on disappeared. The car shot into air and began to fall into the pit of the quarry.

Just before the car hit bottom, Michelle jerked awake. She sat up and turned on the light. After a moment Tommy stepped into the doorway.

"Are you okay?" He asked.

"Yeah. Just caught your bad dream," Michelle said.

"I've started to wonder if I will ever get another good night's sleep," Tommy said.

"I wonder that myself. Like I used to say when I was in college: 'sleep is for the lazy and business majors.' If I keep having that kind of dream, I don't think I want to sleep," she said.

"I've been thinking. I think our better bet is to try and sneak in tonight. I think the storm will decrease the diligence of the surveillance. I hate to wait any longer," Tommy said.

"I'm game. How soon do you want to go?" Michelle asked.

"Now. I put everything we'll need into the car while you were asleep," Tommy said.

"Okay. And just so we are clear, what do we say if we get caught?" Michelle asked.

"I have a feeling that if we get caught and aren't shot on sight, that honesty is gonna be our best policy."

"So what do you think our chances are?" she asked.

"Of getting caught or getting shot?"

"Either."

"If we can get to the tunnel, I'd say pretty good to not get caught. But getting there is maybe fifty-fifty," Tommy said.

Michelle thought for a moment. She was silent as she put her shoes on. She stood and looked at Tommy, studying his face.

"Let's go," she said.

Chapter 39

Hedwick walked close to the rock wall. She approached the corner that would give her the first real look at the object. She could feel her heart pounding. It was the adrenaline surging through her. She was familiar with the feeling. There had been a time in her life, as a teenager, she had sought this feeling.

She edged closer to the corner. The rush of adrenaline brought some of those times back to mind. The sensation was like that of scent memory. Hedwick thought of going skydiving on her sixteenth birthday. She thought about the summer during college, she had spent chasing tornadoes in Oklahoma and Kansas with her uncle the meteorology professor.

Then another memory came up that did not fit. Unfortunately, it came almost every time the rush of adrenalin hit her. It came unbidden and very much unwelcome. She was seventeen and it was her first kiss. The rush had been the same. She remembered every detail. Her heart had pounded and her face had flushed. She felt like she had been falling from the airplane again. It was always a bittersweet memory because her heart had been broken shortly after that. The boy had reveled himself to be a typical teenage boy, with typical teenage boy motivations and typical teenage boy desires. She had been unwilling. She had ended their last encounter with some of the karate she her brother had taught her after his second tour with the marines. This had gained her a reputation. It was one she could be proud of instead of one she would be ashamed of. It had also kept her from getting any more dates until she went to college. She had decided that it was better to be regarded with fear than lust.

In college her favorite adrenaline rush was skateboarding on the parking ramp. She would try to time her runs to get as close as possible to the cars on the street when she left the ramp. The louder the drivers honked and the fouler their language, the bigger the rush. It ended after Hedwick had gotten hit by a car and spent two weeks in the hospital. That had cured her desire for adrenaline.

She was nearly to the corner that would allow her to see the object with her own eyes.

"I'm at the corner," Hedwick said.

"Good. Take a look around the corner and tell us what you see," Robert said in her ear.

"Okay." Hedwick inched closer to the edge. She peered around the corner.

There ahead of her was the thing. It looked almost exactly as it did in the monitors in the cage. The one exception was that the dark opening with the bright spot in the middle had grown.

The storm broke at that instant. Rain came in a torrent. Hedwick felt soaked through almost instantly. Her radio was waterproof, so she could hear Robert when he asked, "Are you still with me?"

"Yeah. It looks the same. The light in the middle looks brighter, that's all." She said.

A bolt of lighting struck the rim of the far side of the quarry. For a moment, the image of an exploding tree was burned into Hedwick's retinas. A second later the sharp crack beat into her ears. For a moment she was stunned. Her senses were completely overloaded. The hair stood up on her neck and on her arms. The earpiece of the radio crackled.

"…Hedwick! Are you all right?" Robert yelled.

She came back to herself in a moment when she heard his voice. "Yeah. I… I think I'm okay. Just a little stunned. Man that was close," she said.

"Oh my god!" Robert said.

Hedwick looked back around the corner. The image projected by the object was moving. The lightning had apparently disrupted whatever system the thing used to project its image. Hedwick knew, though, that was not what caused Robert to react.

Moving away from the opening on the object was a shape. More accurately, it was the total lack of shape. It was black, but not the black of night or the black of new asphalt or the black of flat paint. It was a hole in reality. There was no reflection. There was absolutely noting visible except for the nothingness. It was more than a shadow. Hedwick became terrified as she watched it move. It reminded her of the tales she had heard of the shadow people. They had been described like this in the ghost stories she had heard at summer camp from her friends late at night in the cabin. This gave her an adrenalin rush unlike any she could remember. The terror was total. The danger seemed completely real. There was no safety net for this. There was no parachute. The shape—or more exactly the shape of the hole—was that of a person.

Chapter 40

Michelle and Tommy loaded a couple bottles of water into the car. Tommy got the pistol from his trunk, and loaded it.

"I hope you don't need that," Michelle said.

"So do I. But, I'd rather have it and not need it, than need it and not have it," Tommy answered. "I think our best bet is to go straight north from here up to Canal and then drive east. There is a woods about half a mile west of where we need to go. I think we can get to the old canal ditch from there without being seen."

"Alright. Let's go over it again: what is our story if we get caught? That is, if they don't kill us right away. We should know what we are going to say," Michelle said.

"Well. I suppose go with the obvious. Say you are a reporter and you were trying to get the story. And I'm an on again off again boyfriend who is helping. The simpler the story, the easier to sell. And if that fails, go with complete honesty," Tommy said.

"Alright. I'm ready."

They drove out of the barn. Tommy closed the door. The rain had slowed to a drizzle. The lightning had moved to the north and east, although the rumble of thunder could still be heard in the distance. Tommy guessed it would be raining at the quarry now. He hoped that would help them sneak in.

They drove north to the Canal road. The rain became heavier as they drove north. They turned east, toward the quarry. The rain grew steadily heavier as they approached.

Tommy pulled onto a path that went into a heavy woods. Tommy had played here growing up. Billie French had lived across the road. Tommy and Billie spent many hours playing Robin Hood and Treasure Hunt and Hide-and-Seek in these woods. They had built a tree house in the Y of a gigantic cottonwood tree near the edge of the woods. That tree house had served as pirate ship, club house and in the fall it doubled as a deer blind.

The trees here had never been logged. There were several ancient oak and hickory trees. Tommy, in the summer after getting out of the army, had spent many hours in these woods. The energy of the old trees and the smell of the rotting leaves made him think about how the awful things he had seen would not matter to these trees, that would still be standing long after he was gone. The thought that those things did not matter to something living made him think that, perhaps it was possible someday they might matter less to him. Tommy cut off the engine and the lights.

"This is it," he said and opened his door.

He tucked the pistol into the back of his pants. He hung the binoculars around his neck. He chugged a bottle of water and looked across the top of the Chevelle to Michelle.

"Are you ready?" he asked. "I've got a feeling that this is going to be over quickly. I don't know how it is going to go, but when the time comes, trust your instincts."

They walked slowly back up the path to the edge of the woods. Even though the rain had slackening, by the time they reached the road they were soaked.

Tommy paused. He looked toward the quarry through the binoculars. He watched for almost a minute. He could see nothing that caused alarm. There were no vehicle lights along the road.

"I think we're clear. After the next crossroad, we need to get down into the canal bed. It is probably going to be tough going and muddy, but it should help to hide us most of the way. And, we have to stay as quiet as possible," Tommy said.

"Alright. I'm ready," Michelle said.

They walked to the crossroad, then climbed down into the canal. About halfway down, Tommy slipped. He slid down to the bottom of the ditch. He began to laugh. He could not help himself. It was the sound he made when he hit bottom. He had breathed out a heavy "Ooof." At the same time, his butt hit the soft muck. It made a wet squishing noise in the mud.

Michelle scrambled down next to him. She was laughing too. She sat down by him. Sitting in the mud, for a moment they laughed together. It was much needed stress relief prior to stepping into the unknown.

"I didn't realize how much I needed that," Tommy finally said.

"Now we need to be quiet."

Tommy stood and helped Michelle up. The rain was now only a

light drizzle. They began to walk toward the quarry. From that angle, low in the canal bed, they could see the tree that Tommy had pointed out earlier, silhouetted against the lights from the quarry.

"That is where we need to go," Tommy whispered.

Michelle nodded.

They moved slowly. The bottom of the canal held some water most of the time. The rain had made the muck deeper and softer than usual.

As they walked, Michelle thought about the reason this canal had been dug in the first place, 150 years before. She had written several articles over the last few years about the canal and had researched its history. She realized suddenly they were near the place where the Reservoir War had been fought. The farmers, whose land had been flooded by the government to provide the reservoir for this portion of the canal, decided to revolt. The local constabulary sided with the farmers, who were also their families and neighbors. By the time the federal officials and company representatives arrived, the reservoir was empty and the earthen dam had been completely leveled. The company had lost money on this section of the canal prior to this time and never rebuilt the reservoir. It was one of the last events in the death of the canal system in this part of the state.

As she walked in the mud, it occurred to her she was the great-great-granddaughter of one of those farmers. The story had been told over and over at family reunions and Christmas parties her entire life. It was only one of the colorful local legends that had involved her ancestors.

They walked slowly in the mud. The silhouette of the tree grew steadily larger. Michelle had not realized how huge the tree was. It had seemed just another tree when seen from the road. As they approached on foot, the canopy blocked out the sky. The trunk seemed a pillar of a giant monument more than a tree.

"Well, here we are. You can stay here or come with me. That's your choice. The opening of the tunnel is about seventy-five feet from here," Tommy said.

"I'm coming with you. I can't just sit here and wait."

"Okay."

They climbed out of the canal bed and began to move through the darkness toward where Tommy hoped he would be able to find the opening of the tunnel.

Chapter 41

"Hedwick, get back here!" Robert shouted.

At the same moment the rain began to fall in heavy drops. The wind had began to whip, where it had been calm just moments earlier. The rain, as Hedwick took a last, brief glance around the corner, looked like the sheets that had hung on the clothes line in the backyard when she was a child.

A line from "Our Town" came to mind. She could not remember it exactly, but it was something about how, for three days, the rain looked like sheets blowing down main street. She had been in the play in high school. But very little of it had stuck with her other than the image painted by those words.

She turned and ran back toward the cage. She was soaked through before she was a quarter of the way back. The rain was coming at such an angle the rock wall beside which she ran offered no protection. When she reached the cage her matted hair was plastered against her head and her shoes squished when she moved. The rain was a cold contrast to the heat of the rocks and air. By the time she stepped into the relative shelter of the cage, she was all gooseflesh.

She pulled off the headset and the box on her belt. She moved close to Robert. He was watching the monitor of the camera on top of the outcropping. The figure moved slowly in a line, almost directly toward BARRy. It moved like a person.

Every science fiction movie Hedwick had ever seen flashed in bits and pieces, jumbled together, through her mind. This was the moment where the... Monster, alien, zombie... enemy was revealed: "Klatu verata nictu." "Luke, I am your father." "She can't take any more captain." "That's not a moon, it's a battle station." "He's dead Jim."

Hollywood had not prepared her for what happened next. The figure reached a point just outside the imaginary perimeter. The figure's right hand reached and touched its left forearm. The shadow wavered for a moment. A man appeared. Just a man. It was not a monster, or an alien.

The man was large and heavy. He was dressed in white pants and a white shirt. This image from the camera was not distinct enough to see him clearly, but the three in the cage were suddenly not as afraid as they had been a moment earlier.

The man moved over to BARRy, again touching his left forearm. The monitors showing BARRy's camera images flashed to life. The robot began its routine for returning to the cage. The figure walked calmly by its side as the robot turned and rolled slowly toward the corner of the outcropping of limestone.

Just before BARRy pulled around the corner, it stopped.

They watched as the figure stepped into the line of sight of the robot's cameras. The image now on the monitor was much clearer than what they had seen on the security camera.

The man—for there could no longer be any doubt it was a man—looked to be in his thirties. He wore his hair in a close buzz cut that only partially disguised his receding hairline. He was clean shaven and pale. The shirt was unadorned except for a small equilateral triangle surrounding a lowercase letter "t", embroidered on the collar just below the man's Adam's apple. He had blue eyes, a deep blue with a rim at the outer edge of the iris that was cobalt. Hedwick was comforted by these eyes. They were not the eyes of a monster. Robert felt at ease as well when he looked into them. There was an almost palpable intelligence and gentleness there.

Other than the eyes, his face was completely unremarkable. There were the earliest hints of crow's feet at the corners of the eyes and a very slight furrow in the brow. These seemed not to give the appearance of age or sadness, but to indicate that there had once been worry and concern in the face that were now a thing of the past.

Sue reserved judgment. She was struck by the fact that he was completely dry, even thought the rain had not yet stopped.

He waited, standing still and looking directly into the camera. It was only about ten seconds. To Robert, Sue and Hedwick, it seemed an eternity.

Then he smiled and began to speak.

Chapter 42

Tommy stopped suddenly after they had gone about thirty feet from the canal and listened. He thought he had heard something moving ahead of him. As he waited he heard a soft foot step in the mud ahead. It was not the sound of a human. He moved forward slowly and was startled as several wild turkeys took off at a trot, gobbling loudly.

"Holy Crap," he whispered.

Michelle let out a little yelp. "That was too much. If we get out of this I'm having turkey every week 'til they are all dead."

"I'm with you on that. I think I can see the tunnel opening up there. This is it," he said.

They moved slowly toward the depression where they expected to find the opening to the shaft that would lead them into the quarry.

There was a grill of heavy wire set in the opening of the tunnel. It was rusty but a sign was there, shining in the dim light. Tommy flipped on his flashlight and covered the lens with his hand. He let a sliver of light escape, to assess how best to remove the grate. The sign attached to the grill read:

Property of Shawnee Inc.

Trespassers will be Prosecuted

Tommy pulled on the grate. To his surprise, it moved easily. Only its own weight and a bit of overgrowth had been holding it in place.

Tommy held the flashlight down into the opening and let the full beam of the light shine. The tunnel dropped straight down about thirty feet. There were rungs of rusted rebar embedded into the wall opposite from Tommy. On the side 90° to the left of the ladder rungs an eight inch pipe rose from the depths of the tunnel. Tommy knew it led all the way to the little pump house on the edge of the pond at the bottom of the pit. This pipe went through the side of the tunnel about six feet below the opening. It headed back underground, the way Tommy and Michelle had come, to the Canal where it emptied.

Tommy knew the tunnel sloped away from the bottom of the shaft he was looking down. It ran about 350 feet toward the pit before it dropped the final forty feet, to the rough opening behind the pump house.

In high school, that sloping section of tunnel occasionally held illicit parties. There had even been a keg of beer lowered down the tunnel with ropes. One of the attendees had gotten busted by her parents and spilled the location of the kegger. That had been the end of the tunnel parties. For several years there had been a lock on the tunnel opening and routine checks by the Sherriff's department. The checks had slackened over time, but as far as Tommy knew there had never been any more parties in the tunnel. He thought ruefully that, now, there likely never would be.

Tommy went around to the side of the opening with the ladder. He swung his legs over the edge and began to climb down. Once he was far enough in, he paused and held the light so Michelle could see the top rungs. She began to descend as well. They climbed silently to the bottom of the first vertical shaft. They were breathing hard and not entirely due to the physical exertion.

"So far so good," Michelle said.

"Yep. I hope the rest goes as smoothly. The tunnel will slope down from here and curve to the left up ahead. We want to be careful we don't accidentally fall into the shaft at the other end of the tunnel." Tommy said.

"I know that. I came to a party or two out here, back in the day," Michelle said.

"I forgot that you used to run with that crowd," Tommy said. He laughed softly. The sound echoed loudly on the hard stone of the tunnel walls.

"Let's try to be a little more quiet, shall we?" Michelle said in her best imitation of a puckered up school marm.

'Yes ma'am," Tommy said.

He shone the light down the tunnel to where the curve of the walls blocked their line of sight. They began to walk, making little sound as they went. Soon they made the final turn to where they could see the hole of the lower shaft.

Tommy had half expected to see some of the MP's waiting for them. There were none. The whole time they were walking, he had expected footsteps from behind. There had been none. Meeting no resistance thus far gave him a nervous confidence. He edged up to the hole of the lower shaft and peered over. He strained his ears and heard nothing but the low hum of the pumps far below.

"Last chance to turn back," Tommy said.

"Nope. Besides, call me lazy but I'd rather climb down than up," she said.

With that, Tommy swung his legs over the edge and began the final descent into the quarry.

Chapter 43

The man smiled. His teeth were very white. They were perfect. Despite this perfection, the smile was genuine. It was comforting and friendly. Robert, Hedwick and Sue were not afraid. Robert wondered if that was because there was really nothing to fear. Or if it was due to something the man was doing to control their fears.

"Hello. My name is Jonathan Irons. I am sure you have many questions. Let me assure you that those questions will be answered in time. I have much to tell you first. I wish for you to come and visit with me where I am. For reasons you will understand soon, I must remain within the line of sight of my vessel. I know that your robot has speakers that you can use to speak to me. I know you can hear me."

He paused. Sue scrambled and flipped a couple switches. She spoke into her own headset.

"We are here. You have our undivided attention. Why are you here? Where are you from? How…"

"Sue, I understand your impatience. Your questions will be answered. Will you come out to me? It will make our conversation much easier," Jonathan said.

Sue was stunned. How did he know her name? A million more questions ran through her mind. The same questions were in the minds of Robert and Hedwick.

"There is one thing that I need to have addressed immediately. In about ten minutes, there will be a man and a woman who will emerge from the tunnel behind the pump house beside the pond at the bottom of the pit. Please send someone there to meet them and bring them here. They are not to be harmed. Please make the call, Robert."

Robert picked up a radio and sent a pair of guards. Then he picked up a headset and put it on.

"You absolutely have the upper hand here. I assume you know much more about us than our names. I also assume if your intentions were hostile we would already be dead, or prisoners. We have learned enough about your technology to know that. We will come out there to you. Give us a few moments," Robert said.

"Very well. You will not need your weapons. Hedwick, that includes the knife you have on your ankle. I will wait for you. We have much to discuss," Jonathan said. He smiled again at the camera. He reached forward. The monitors went black.

Hedwick reached down to her left ankle and removed the blade that was there. She unclipped her gun belt and placed it on the counter, near the back of the cage. There was something about the man that made her feel as if she had no option to disobey.

Robert hesitated for a moment, wondering whether he really wanted to meet an unknown without protection. Then his own words came to him. "He could have already destroyed us." He unclipped his gun belt as well. He felt no fear. As strange as this situation was, as many unknowns that were involved, the hesitation and the low thrum of anxiety that was almost always present in the back of his mind were gone. He was not sure if it was because there was nothing to fear or if he was being manipulated. Whatever the reason, he wasn't afraid.

Sue never carried a weapon. At least not a lethal weapon. She had occasionally been known to carry a Taser. It was more for her own entertainment than for protection. She had been known to zap the profoundly egotistical jerks she encountered at scientific meetings she frequented. Some of the big names in physics tended to get much too full of themselves at the open bar mixers after hours at the conferences. These same big names would resort to name calling and psychological attacks when Sue would poke a hole in their latest theory. Sue would often continue to bait them until they either threatened or actually acted violence against her. Then she would zap them, often to applause. Sue did not have a Taser now. She also believed she would not need it, and that she would have difficulties poking holes in anything this man would be telling her. There was something very believable and genuine about this man.

Jonathan Irons stood waiting. His mission had already been a success. If it had not, he could not be standing here at all. He knew this success would continue. His standing here was evidence of his future success. That would be the hardest part to make them understand. He knew Sue would grasp it immediately. Robert and

Hedwick would take longer. Tommy would never fully understand all of the truth. But Jonathan did not need him to understand, just to believe. Michelle would believe, but also would never totally understand all the details. She was smart, but the deep technical part of how he was here was beyond her experience. She did not need to understand it all to believe.

Jonathan thought about the long period of preparation that brought him to this place. He knew he would be here only a short time, compared to those years. This was the reason for his life's work. He knew the next few minutes, when he met these people he knew everything about, would be the most exciting of his life.

Chapter 44

Michelle hated the feeling of fear that confronted her when she had to swing her legs out over the unknown, gaping hole in order to put her feet on the ladder. Once she was on the ladder she was fine. The regularity and stability of the rungs calmed her. It was getting her feet out onto the first rung that took all of her courage.

Each time she had to get onto a ladder from the top she thought about the one time it had gone badly. She had been a tomboy growing up. Her brothers had often taken advantage of this to dare her into stunts that would have made her mother prematurely gray. This time had been like all the others. She was supposed to climb up a ladder onto the barn roof to retrieve the Frisbee she and her brothers had been playing with. She had had no problem scampering up the ladder. She had edged out onto the barn roof, retrieved the Frisbee and thrown it down to her brothers.

When she had gone to get back onto the ladder, something had gone wrong. Perhaps the base of the ladder was too close to the barn. Maybe Michelle had been clumsy. To Michelle it did not really matter. All she could remember was, the instant she had put all of her weight on the ladder, it had started to tip away from the barn. Michelle had fallen almost twenty feet. She had broken both bones in her left forearm. Ever since, when getting on a ladder, she felt that same moment of fear.

She had been reminded about that fear as she climbed down the ladder. She had been lost in her own thoughts. She almost did not realize when Tommy stopped below her. She only noticed because he flipped off the light.

"What?' Michelle whispered.

Tommy heard fear in her voice, partially because of the ladder phobia and partially because she did not know why Tommy had turned off the light.

"I heard something below us." Tommy whispered.

Michelle could barely hear him. She strained. She heard nothing for a moment, then muffled voices. She could not make out any words. She also heard a fainter noise, the crunch of feet on gravel. Who ever was down there was not taking any measures to hide their approach. To Michelle, that meant that either they knew that she and Tommy were there and did not expect any trouble, or they were out on a routine check of the quarry and did not expect to find anyone.

Michelle weighed both of these possibilities. She could not decide which scenario was more likely. She finally decided that the only way to find out was to go further down the ladder. She was about to try to convey this to Tommy when she heard a voice from below.

"We know you are up there. Come down slowly. You will not be hurt," the voice said.

A bright light shined up from below. Michelle looked away for an instant, blinded. She knew they could see Tommy and her. The fact they were not already dead gave her a small glimmer of hope.

"I have a pistol in my belt. I am going to leave it there while I climb down. When I reach the bottom, my hands will remain on the ladder until you instruct me to proceed," Tommy said.

Michelle had forgotten about the gun. That could have gone badly. She was glad Tommy had thought of it. It would have been terrible to have come this far and get killed because of a misunderstanding.

"Come down slowly. The man comes first. Ma'am, stay put for now. Good," the voice said.

Michelle held fast to the rungs. She was afraid to move. Tommy began to climb down slowly. It seemed like forever to Michelle before she heard Tommy's boots crunch in the gravel at the bottom of the tunnel.

"Sir. I'm going to come remove the pistol from your belt. My partner has you covered. So please, no sudden moves," the voice said.

Then Michelle heard footsteps on the gravel. Then the click and ratchet as the unknown person ejected the magazine and the chambered round from Tommy's gun.

"Step over here please," The voice said faintly. Then louder, "Ma'am, please come down slowly. Keep your hands on the last rung when your reach the bottom. You will be checked for weapons."

Michelle climbed down. This time the wait seemed much shorter. Her mind was focused on not falling. The last step onto solid ground surprised her. She held onto the rung. The person attached to the voice came up and ran a magnetic wand over her body, looking for weapons. Then she heard the crunch of gravel as the soldier stepped back.

"Very well. Both of you come with us," the voice said.

"Where are we going?" Michelle asked.

"There is someone who wants to meet you. That is all I can say."

Chapter 45

Robert and Hedwick began to walk out of the cage immediately. Sue took a moment to be sure all of the information that would be coming at them soon would be recorded. As good as her memory was, she wanted to be sure she did not miss anything.

"Come on," Robert said.

"Just a second. You'll thank me later," Sue said.

She flipped a couple of switches then headed toward the other two. She was excited to learn everything she could about the technology this person represented. She hoped he had a deep understanding of that technology. Sue would rather talk to a rocket scientist over an astronaut. Astronauts were not stupid. They simply had too many other responsibilities to truly understand all of the detailed theory behind every bit of the technology that thrust them into space. The scientists often had a more limited scope of duty and experience than the astronauts, but the depth of their knowledge was always more interesting to Sue. She knew that her first few questions of this person would make it clear quickly with which she was dealing. As she thought this, a line from the song "Rocket Man" came to mind:

"All this science I can't understand

It's just my job five days a week."

She smiled an enigmatic smile for a moment, then joined Robert and Hedwick.

The three walked quickly along the rock wall. They tried to not show the excitement they felt. Robert knew this was beyond any human experience. He knew that the next hour would make an incredible change in the course of human history, the course of humanity itself. He hoped it was for the better. Unlike Sue, he was hoping to be given broad strokes of the basic answers to his questions. The depth of knowledge Sue had acquired regarding several subjects was simply beyond Robert. He knew this. He understood the basics, but the deep theory simply was too much for him. Often it was the point at which an idea could no longer be described in words and required complex mathematics for accurate description, that he lost the ability to follow a subject. This helped him to value others according to their different skills.

Hedwick walked quietly. She wanted to know so much from this man. She wanted to know why the men who had been boiled by that object had to die. She wanted to know the answers to impossible questions. Every question for her was shaded by the human element. She had almost always based her decisions on what would provide the greatest benefit to others. Even when she had been forced to kill, she had thought about the weight of that death versus the deaths that might result from her inaction.

Without a word, they stopped when they reached the corner. After only a moment's hesitation, Robert took the first step around the corner.

Robert was surprised by what he saw. The first thing he had noticed was that the man was larger than he had expected. Robert guessed he was just over six feet tall and broad across the shoulders. His attire reminded Robert of a Karate outfit without a belt. He guessed the man to weigh close to 300 pounds, but he did not appear to have any fat on him. Robert realized he had subconsciously associated the man with being the pilot of the object. In Robert's experience, pilots—at least military pilots—were built smaller than this man. It was the incongruity of Robert's idea of a pilot and the man's massive form that had caused the surprise.

The three walked forward until they stood about ten feet from the man. He quietly raised his hand for them to stop. The action was firm but not threatening.

"I know you are anxious to begin, but let us wait just a few minutes until the other two arrive. I do not wish to explain the same things multiple times." Jonathan said.

The path on which the guards took Tommy and Michelle wound steeply up from the pump house. It had many switchbacks and went up to the top of the quarry and led them onto the gravel yard on the side opposite the office building at the main part of the pit. There was no direct line of sight from that path to the object that they knew was there.

The guards took them back across the yard, past the building and they walked down into the pit, and past the cage. Once they reached the end of the limestone wall, they stopped.

"Go around the corner," one of the guards said.

Tommy and Michelle turned the corner and stood speechless. The scale of the object was incredible. Tommy was struck by the minuteness of the four human figures, about thirty yards ahead of them, in comparison to the object that was further away. It reminded him of the first time he had stood on the deck of an aircraft carrier.

The feeling of the huge discrepancy in size was something that Michelle had never experienced to this degree. The only thing that came close was when she had stepped onto the field of the old Hoosier Dome during a sports reporting class in college.

One of the figures looked toward them. He smiled.

"Please, come join us. We have important things to discuss," he said.

Michelle and Tommy were powerless to resist. They began to walk toward the other people.

Chapter 46

"There, now our little group is complete," Jonathan said as Tommy and Michelle joined the others.

"Tommy, Michelle, I am Jonathan Irons. Tommy, I am a relative of yours. I was named after your great-grandfather. These are Sue, Hedwick and Robert," he said.

Then to the others, "These are Tommy Irons and Michelle Perry."

The five stood silent. They each had so many questions running through their minds. They found it almost impossible to decide which to ask first.

Finally, Michelle broke the silence. "You have us at a distinct disadvantage. You seem to know more about us than we know about you." She said.

"Very true." Jonathan said. "The question is where to begin, with purpose then explanation; or explanation then conclude with purpose. That is always the question. Fortunately I know the answer. I believe explanation then purpose is best. Bear with me Sue. I believe you're going to be a step ahead most of the time with much of this, but I need to be sure my explanations are as clear as possible.

Sue nodded slightly. She was used to being ahead of many of the conversations that went on around her.

"I just want to know why you are here and who you are." Robert said. It came out a bit harsher than he had intended. He immediately felt self-conscious, even a little embarrassed. It was a sensation he had not experienced in a long time. Once he realized what he was feeling, instead of being angry with himself, or feeling more embarrassed, he was amused. A slight smile curled up at the corners of his mouth.

"In good time, Robert. Let me first assure you all, that each of you has a role here. It is not by chance that you are here. Let that suffice for now on that front. The reasons for each of you to be here are different. I will explain them to each of you.

"Please sit." Jonathan waved his hand in a broad arc toward some blocks of stone just behind them. He sat on a block near which he had been standing. The other five sat as well.

"Good. I'll begin my explanation by asking you a question. Which of you believe in the possibility of time travel?" Jonathan asked.

They sat there mute, stunned by the question. After a brief moment. Sue began to smile. She raised her hand. She began to see a light dawning on what was going on in the pit. She had several questions spring to mind. Most of the questions were technical. The one question that came around time and again amongst all the many others was, "Why?"

Robert was in disbelief of the question. He had read briefs on the subject. It seemed technologically impossible. Then he saw Sue's hand raise. He had never known her to believe in the impossible. His faith in Sue was enough to make up his mind. His own hand raised.

Hedwick's hand had been the first to go up. She had always felt that there should be a way to travel in time. It was, after all, a fact that we were all time travelers. It just happened that we could presently perceive time traveling in one direction. Everything else in nature and chemistry worked in reversible processes. Chemical reactions could be reversed. Even nuclear reactions could be reversed with the application of enough energy. For Hedwick, there was nothing to say that time must be one directional. At least Hedwick had never heard any good argument that went beyond the idea that observation and perception constitute the whole of reality. Therefore, since humans simply could not perceive time going backward and it could not be scientifically observed, it must be impossible. Just because humans were wired, created or evolved to experience time in one direction, did not imply to her it was the only way in which time must necessarily be experienced. She had flashes of several late night, beer-fuelled discussions along these lines with the physics majors who had lived across the hall from her in the dorms

She did believe in the linearity of time. At least in the sense that events were next to each other temporally were always so and other events could not, on the deep levels of time, be interjected between those events if they did not actually occur then.

Tommy looked puzzled. He had always thought about things in a black and white way. Time travel had always seemed so gray to him. All the time travel movies he had seen had left him in a vicious cycle of cause and effect. He has stopped watching movies like that after the first Terminator movie. He had gotten flummoxed by the idea that the technology that had made the Terminator possible was the Terminator itself. The logical contradiction made it aggravating for him to think about.

Tommy had a momentary pang as he remembered when he had taken Cindy to the drive-in in Ashap to watch the movie. Tommy had intended it to be a typical make out session, as it had been several times before. However, they actually watched the movie. It had hooked Tommy almost from the start. He had watched, intrigued by the special effects and the story. After it was over his mind started to try and reason out how exactly that sort of time travel would work. Every time he thought too long about it, his mind got stuck in loops.

Despite these doubts, after a moment, Tommy raised his hand. Partly it was because of the raised hands of the others. A good portion, however, was due to the thought that asking about time travel in this situation would be very strange indeed, if in fact it was not directly bearing on what was happening. Tommy could not deny the evidence of his own eyes that the object was directly in front of him. And since time travel had been suggested, it must be a possibility.

Michelle had quickly raised her hand. Time travel was something she had always wanted to believe in. She had never really looked deeply into the physics of it, of the principles of how causality was dealt with in theory. There was something about it that simply appealed to her. Oddly enough that appeal was due not so much to the romance of time travel itself, but to the idea that it would allow for space travel, over profound distances, to be more practical.

She remembered, when she was in high school, learning about travel at the speed of light. Her teacher had said that one could travel a large portion of the speed of light, but that, due to time dilation, by the time the traveler got anywhere interesting there would be no one around to tell about it. Time on earth would move so much faster than it did for the traveler. That idea had bothered Michelle. It seemed so wrong to her that such great discoveries could never be shared.

The answer had come to her one night during the following

summer. She and a couple of her girlfriends had borrowed Michelle's father's pickup truck and driven out to a clearing in the big woods north of the river. The sky had been crystal clear, and the stars were incredibly bright. Her friend Juli had repeated a phrase from science class.

"The light from those stars that we are seeing now left those stars millions of years ago."

The light had flickered on for her. Michelle realized that if one could travel back in time, after a trip to the stars, then the time dilation would not matter. Of course she had never really thought it was possible. But it was a solution to the problem that she had not heard of elsewhere.

Jonathan looked around the circle of raised hands and smiled.

"Good. That will make this a little easier," he said.

Chapter 47

William watched the terminal. He was trying desperately to process what had happened over the last thirty minutes. There was so much new information. Two things kept circling one another in his mind.

The first was the introduction of these two new people. Why were they here? Why had Robert let them come in, simply at a word from the man from the...

That was the second point that was circling his brain. He had been convinced that this thing was an alien ship. When the shape came out, he was expecting contact with an alien race. Time travel had simply not crossed his mind as an explanation. Humans being responsible for it seemed somehow even more difficult to believe.

The first problem was difficult. Why were they not detained? What worried William more was how they got past the security measures. He had personally checked over the blueprints and plans of the plant. Everything had been covered. He knew he would be to blame for these people getting in here. Was there a problem with the personnel? These were the questions he had been trying to answer, when the Man had dropped the time travel bomb. Somehow, because of that connection, the two things seemed to be interlocked in his mind.

He knew that he had to find out where the security failure was. But he was beginning to realize that there might be a way to use these intruders to help him when he released the information he had been gathering. Perhaps he could even use these two to do it for him. That would entail him getting them the information and convincing them that they must keep the source secret. It was an interesting possibility.

The man had said that each of them in the pit had a role. What could the two civilians possibly have to do with the operation? The level of clearance that would be necessary to even know about that thing was staggering. It seemed impossible that civilians with unchecked backgrounds could have any possible role to play in anything that might be going on.

This was an enormous advance. Time travel was something out of fiction. It was not supposed to be possible. There was much more legitimate evidence for extraterrestrials than there was for time travel. It started to dawn on him that this was perhaps bigger than aliens after all.

The technical questions began to surface in his thoughts, but William suppressed them. He knew that Sue would have a much better grasp on that part of things than he would, at least initially. He would be more than willing to spend the time talking to her to get a good understanding of it when he had a chance. For now, the "how" was simply not relevant to William's purpose. He refocused on his overriding goal. He needed the evidence to blow this open. He checked to be sure the feeds from the cage were still recording. He was satisfied to see they were, and that there was sufficient memory to record several more hours.

William wondered if the man knew of a role for him. Was there some information that the man in the pit had that would condemn him? William hoped that he would be able to get out of this. He realized that his own position had suddenly become precarious. He would have to watch and listen very closely to what was said. He began to think of how he might escape if it appeared he would be caught. He had made plans for just such a possibility long ago. He was confident he could readily disappear if he needed to. He would prefer to see this through. He wanted to see what was going to happen with the machine and the new people.

He began to gather himself and focus back on what was going on in the pit. He was a little upset that he was not out there himself. He realized that he was a victim of his own tactics. He had played the game and made it appear that he was not particularly creative, but just good at problem solving. He realized that Hedwick and Robert had gone out there because they were leaders. William had never shown any real leadership qualities. They were out there and he was not. That simple fact made William realize that he wanted to expose all of this, more than he had ever wanted anything. It was so close. He had to be careful.

He turned back to the monitor and watched. He listened. He waited.

Chapter 48

Jonathan paused for a moment. He knew what he would say. He just wanted to savor this moment. This was, after all, a historic moment—at least it was in his history. This was the point in which the course of his life would be set, before he was born. At the same time it would affect his future in ways he was unable to tell: or at least he had not been informed yet of how this would affect his future. The future from this point to his present was known. It was what was after this point—in his present—that was unknown. He tried to not think about that too much. Despite the years of theoretical physics, and an understanding of the "how", the implications and the "Keeping Things Straight" always stretched him.

"The first answer is, yes. I am from the future, your future," he said with an emphasis on "your".

The last part of the statement was for Sue's benefit. As part of his preparation for this moment, he had read all of Sue's scientific publications. Some, those outside his area of expertise, were a bit beyond him. Others, although cutting edge when published, were hopelessly antiquated. There were a couple papers on the theory of time travel. In those one of the theories Sue had written about was the possibility of time travel into the past being only possible if that travel was into another reality in a multiverse setting. That is, it might be possible to travel into someone else's past reality, but not the traveler's own past. Of course he knew that was not true.

"What you see, the object out there, is the time machine. It is not really here. For that matter, neither am I. It is a projection from the future. I am a projection, from the projection. But we will talk about that and the specifics of how it works later." He looked at Sue directly as he said this. "Right now I want to talk more about why I am here."

Sue's brain was whirring. Of course. Projection instead of actual presence made perfect sense. The principle made sense. She was interested in how it worked, but the question of what was, in the global perspective, more important. Her own interests could wait.

"This contact is the first of its kind. At least when viewed from my present. There will be, in my future, projections further back in time. This is the first in the series of experiments. My purpose here is two fold. First, I need your help for this to work. I need you all to play a role. Second—and this is most important. I offer you a gift," Jonathan said.

"The roles you will play are important. We will talk about those roles later, one on one. It is the gift I wish to talk about now. Imagine living your life in complete confidence that your decisions will always be correct? Imagine the freedom with which that would allow you to live. How many times in your lives have you looked back and doubted a decision even though it felt right at the time? How many times have you wished you could change something you have done? The fact that I stand here tells you that all of your decisions, up to the point in time of my present, are the correct decisions, consistent with a future that leads to this moment. If they were not, my existence would never occur and I would not be here now. I give you the gift of living completely in the moment." Jonathan said.

He let this sink in. He could see that all of them were lost in their own thoughts. He did not give them long to think about it though.

"You will find your roles in the future are deeply connected to this gift. Each of you will choose and do things you would not believe possible now. I want to be clear. This does not mean that there will not be responsibility and consequences from your actions. But, with the knowledge that your decisions will be the right ones, living on gut instincts without second guessing will become a way of life.

"This freedom is incredible. I have been living with this freedom for quite a number of years. The fact that this meeting was recorded was evidence to me that each of my decisions would be the correct ones to lead to this day. It is a wonderful way to live."

He smiled. It was a genuine open smile. He had reached the point he had really been looking forward to, because he knew this moment would change many lives beyond those of the five people before him.

"You have all had a long day. Sue, please stay here with me. We have much to speak of that would not be of interest of the others. The rest of you..." He looked at the others. "Please go. Get some rest. I know you all have many questions. I will spend time with each of you. For now I want to speak with Sue. I suggest you eat, drink and rest. I understand sleep will be difficult, but please rest. I will have you each come out in turn. Then we will have more time together as a group. For now, please leave Sue and me alone. Thank you."

Chapter 49

"Come with me," Hedwick said.

"Yes, there's some food and places to rest in the office building," Robert said.

He began to walk toward the corner of the limestone wall. He looked over his shoulder. Sue nodded at him. He turned back. The others followed. They walked in silence. They were each trying to grasp what they had just been told.

"Sue, I asked to speak to you first because our discussion will be the longest. Much of the technology that will come out of this will come through you, either directly or as a derivative of something you do. Your insight is part of what will make what is to come possible. I know you have many questions so let us begin." Jonathan said.

Sue was somewhat surprised at the abrupt opening for questions. She took a moment to collect her thoughts. She weighed several questions to ask first. She was trying to decide if the why was more important than the how. She had often thought about situations such as this. What would she say if faced with an alien species. Well, that was different. There would very likely be a language barrier which would have to be overcome. She pictured overcoming the language barrier leading naturally into the direction of conversations. This was more difficult; language and learning how to communicate could not be used as a crutch to facilitate the content of that communication. She was struck by inspiration.

"What do you think should be the starting point for our discussion?" She asked.

"I think we should begin by giving you a big picture of why I am here. Without the why, the how is inconsequential. Frosting without cake. Although it would be sweet for you, there would not be a foundation upon which it stood.

"My role here is two fold. The first, and most important, is to begin a revolution in the way people think about their lives and actions. The second is to plant the seed for the technology that allows me to be here. For you, Sue, the broad brushstrokes of the first purpose will be enough. It is the second purpose that will be most important and most interesting to you." Jonathan said.

"Is this revolution going to be violent? I can see the premise you mentioned earlier, of the inherent correctness of an individual's decisions being used as the basis of an argument for might makes right." Sue said.

"There will be those individuals who will justify violence, bigotry and inhumanity using whatever means happen to be convenient. This will be no different. However this revolution will empower individuals with courage to resist those who would be tyrants. That has often been absent in the past when tyrants have attempted to arise. I will not deny that there will be horrible things done, using the argument that it is fate, and therefore 'I can do what I want'. Those who take this approach will be those who fail to understand that even though they are free, they do not live without consequence and responsibility. Those who will try to justify the oppression of others, will have their own arguments backfire on them, due to their own short-sightedness. Be assured that there will be upheaval, but it will be brief and the result will more than make up for the price." Jonathan said.

"So. Telling who will arise to be tyrants, and under what circumstances these individuals will arise won't make any difference in preventing this upheaval? It is the grandmother paradox all over." Sue said.

"Exactly. I'm sure you know about the Novikov self-consistency principle. It doesn't matter what I do or tell you here. If it is not consistent with my own past, I will not exist to come back to this place in time. The fact that I am talking to you proves my past, your present, my present and your future all are a consistent whole." Jonathan said.

"I see. I understand as much about the why as I care to right now. I'm ready to learn about the how. How does that thing…" She pointed to the object. "…project itself and your images to this time?"

"What does that shape suggest to you?" Jonathan asked.

"Uncertain. I am not sure what lies buried in the limestone." Sue answered.

"It is a circle that continues the curve as you see it. It tapers out gradually to a point opposite that which you see at the point of the horns. The thickness at the widest point is about twenty-five meters. The diameter is about 900 meters in total." Jonathan said.

"The majority of it is made from high temperature superconducting magnets. The craft is designed for two purposes. Each of which is essential to its function."

"A particle accelerator?" Sue asked.

"Very good. Yes, that is part of the puzzle. The other part is not so obvious, but no less essential. It begins with a pair of Bose-Einstein condensates with masses in the order of 10 to the 10th power kilograms," Jonathan said. He paused when he saw the astonished look on Sue's face.

"But how? That is orders of magnitude more massive than anything theoretically possible. How far from the future are you?" Sue asked.

"About 104 years in your future. It is the innovations you will conceive that will result in my ability to talk with your right now. But please understand the inspirations our discussion will provide will be only that; inspiration. I will not give you all the answers.

"But, back to what I was saying. Imagine two large Bose-Einstein condensates of the aforementioned mass. They are in a single chamber which is in the shape of a cylinder with spherical ends. Each condensate is held in its own magnetic field. The field on one of the two is reversed causing collapse and a rebound Bose nova. At a precisely controlled instant, as the shock wave from the first condensate collapse reaches the second condensate, the magnetic field on the second condensate is reversed as well. Due to the pressure from the shock wave of the first Bose Nova, the second condensate is unable to re-expand and is further compressed by the shock wave until a critical density is reached, at which time..."

"A black hole is created!" Sue finished Jonathan's thought.

"Yes. Now can you put the two pieces together to figure out how the object works to project information backwards in time?" Jonathan asked.

Sue thought for a moment about all of the time travel theories she knew. And just as Jonathan knew it would, the answer came to her.

"If the black hole is rotating, it is playing the part of a Tippler cylinder. Choosing the right orientation relative to the spin of the black hole, the particles that are in the accelerator can act like a craft winding a spiral around the cylinder. That gets them sent back in time. It is actually interference patterns between the particles that are being sent back in time to form these images."

"Exactly. It is the exposure of the beams directly to the frame dragging effect of the black hole that projects that interference pattern. Getting that part tuned just right and choosing the right vectors of the particle beams is what was, perhaps, the most difficult part of making this work. That has only recently in my time line been accomplished.

"That brings me to the point where I can tell you, these things become possible because of the theories you are going to propose over the next several years. This is the basic premise of the technical part of this. The rest is simply extrapolation and reverse engineering to figure out where to start with your present day technology. Let me reassure you, you are the key to the technology on which all of this is based. But, be confident that it works. This conversation is proof of that. Follow your instincts," Jonathan said.

Sue took a deep breath. She looked again at the object, then tilted her head to the side. A thought struck her suddenly. She understood that the projection to the past by the mechanism she and Jonathan were discussing was possible. Receiving signals from the past, however, would not be possible by the same mechanism.

"This is not really a two way conversation, is it?" she asked.

"No. And so you have come to the first limitation of our method. We, meaning those of us in your future, must rely on historical media to supply the past's part of the conversations. Thank you for turning on your recorders. The projection is in one direction only. But, because we know both what we say and your response, all we, in the future must do is project our part of the conversation. To the others, it will be transparent. Please do not tell them, at least not until they have finished talking with me and the projection is gone. They will think they are talking to me in real time. There is no reason for them to think otherwise. The idea of time projection by itself will be difficult enough for them. Telling them that they aren't really carrying on a conversation with me would add an unnecessary level of complexity."

"I agree." Sue said.

"Of course, in a few years, one of your colleagues will point out the asynchronous nature of these conversations. It can wait 'til then to explain it to the others." Jonathan said.

Sue thought about all she had heard and was silent for a few minutes. Jonathan waited.

"I have a question or two about current research in black holes. Can you answer any of them?" Sue asked.

"Of course."

They spent the next two hours discussing deep, hardcore physics of black holes and white holes. They hashed over black hole entropy and Hawking radiation. They discussed primordial black holes versus those formed by the collapse of stars. When they were finished Sue had a clear understanding of what she was up against and a mental outline of a plan how to accomplish it.

As Sue was about to ask another question, Jonathan held up his hand.

"We could talk all night. I don't doubt that. However time is dwindling. This thing consumes incredible amounts of power to maintain the projection. There are limits of how long that power can be managed. So I really do need to move on and talk to the others. There is just one more thing. William James has been spying on you." Jonathan said.

"Yes, I know. Robert and I have known for over a year. We just haven't been able to figure out why or what his plans are." Sue said.

"He wants to expose everything you have all been doing. He wants to out the whole covert element of governmental operations. You and Robert will need to make a decision about how you are going to handle him. I will not tell you how to handle the situation. But it will need to be decided before what is coming in the next twenty-four hours.

"I want to talk to Robert about this before you mention it to him. But, please be thinking about it. He could end up being an exceptional ally or a ferocious enemy. Of course you and Robert will make the right decision. I think we have spoken long enough. Please send Robert to me."

Chapter 50

As Robert walked, slightly behind the other three, he went over the last 48 hours in his mind. Could it really only be two days since the first call? Now he was faced with the reality of time travel. He had so many questions and was having a difficult time organizing his thoughts.

A conversation he had had with his grandmother many years earlier came to mind. Robert had not thought of that conversation for years, but the memory was as clear as if it was part of the last two days. The crunch of the gravel underfoot again transported him to the back road leading toward his grandmother's home.

"Grandma, today in Sunday school, the teacher talked about how God told the prophets about things that were going to happen in the future." Robert said.

"Yes that's true." His grandmother said.

"But then today the preacher talks, in his sermon, about free will. I don't understand how we can have free will, and God can still know the future."

"That's a very good question."

Robert knew that was his grandmother's response when she either did not know the answer or needed a moment to think. After a moment she continued.

"The best way I can explain it is that God exists outside of time. He can see all of time, all at once. When you get home, there is something you can read that might make it more clear to you," she said.

When they got home, she had pulled a volume from one of the many bookshelves in the house. It was Edwin Abbot's Flat Land. This was Robert's first introduction to abstract thinking. When he had finished reading it, he was able to answer his own question about free will not been contradictory to prophesy.

He stubbed his toe on a rock that was sticking up slightly higher than the surrounding gravel. This brought his mind back to the present. The three others walking with him were silent, lost in their own thoughts.

He thought about what his own role might be in whatever the man in the pit had planned. He quickly came to the conclusion that his role would be little different than what he had been doing before this object appeared. He would be the one that kept things going in the right direction. He would be the one who picked the correct person for each task that would keep it going. The function would not change, it would only be the objective that would be different.

The question became what that objective was to be. Robert could see several possibilities. He weighed each quickly and began to formulate a rough outline of the most likely.

Two possibilities rose to the top of his mental list. The first was that there would need to be, behind the scenes string pulling. His connections would make funding and procurement "off the books" much easier. The second possibility was that there needed to be a face to the operation, to divert the attention away from what was really going on. Robert was a master of both of these gray zone skills.

This day has been full of surprises. Perhaps he was wrong and there was something totally unexpected he would be doing. He did not like the thought. Much like his flashbacks, self-doubt had been occurring more often lately. When he had first started this work, he had never doubted that his course of action was right. A few years ago, after Arizona, he began to have occasional doubts. These doubts had become more frequent lately. He was aware that someday, perhaps soon, this doubt and reduced focus might become dangerous to others or himself. Perhaps what he would be expected to do now would help him avoid that danger.

More than anything though, at this instant he was hungry and thirsty. That also had become more pronounced lately. He had, five years ago, been able to go all day without eating and with little to drink. Now he felt hunger more acutely in much less time. Perhaps it was because he was getting older. Perhaps it was something else. He did not like it. He especially disliked the loss of definition in his midsection. Where once there had been a six pack, there is now simply a trim flat stomach. And he had started to have the slightest bit of softness develop on the inside of his thighs.

He went to the cafeteria and got a snack and water. He just

nodded to the others who had also come into the room for refreshment. He ate quickly and decided to try to rest. He grabbed a sandwich and headed out of the cafeteria.

He went to the office, munching the sandwich on the way. He lay down on the plastic cushions of the sofa. Though he did not expect to sleep, he dozed quickly, then fell into deep slumber.

Chapter 51

Hedwick, Tommy and Michelle stopped into the cafeteria in the office building.

"There are sandwiches in the fridge and the vending machines are open. Help yourself," Hedwick said.

"Okay," Michelle said.

Tommy was quiet for a few minutes while he got something to eat. Robert entered the room. Nodded at them, grabbed some food and left.

"What happened to Gregg Childress?" he asked Hedwick after he sat down with a sandwich and soda. He spoke quietly. There was no tone of anger or accusation in the question.

"Ah. I thought that might come up. He committed suicide," Hedwick said.

"But…"

"I know he was left handed. We have found in his journal that he had been thinking about killing himself for a while, and he wanted to do it to make it look like murder. He couldn't live with the fact that he had killed a woman and little girl. Her husband never tried to get revenge and had even forgiven him. That was the part he found hardest to bear. He couldn't understand that," Hedwick said.

"How did you know that? I've know Gregg for years. He was driving the car that—that killed my wife and daughter. There was more than once I though about killing him those first few weeks. Right after the accident. I did forgive him...." Tommy said. He choked up for a moment. Michelle put her hand on his shoulder.

"I know he was mentally ill, and I had seen what some of his meds did to him. When it came out at the trial that his meds had been changed a couple days before the accident... I had taken some of those drugs myself right after the accident … when I was trying to cope … I knew I wouldn't have been okay driving. He... He was on so much, just to be able to function day to day, that I just couldn't blame him. Part of me wanted to. Part of me wanted to make sense of it and if I could hang the blame on him, at least a little of it, it might make sense. I was in bad shape for a while and not having someone to blame I turned my blame to God." Tommy said.

Hedwick looked down. She could not look at Tommy. She had not expected this. The connection between this man and the dead man had not yet been made. She had had her own struggles with faith, but could not imagine what Tommy had been through. Or for that matter the guilt that Gregg had felt. Hedwick had killed. But it was always on purpose and always "VBP". She had started using that abbreviation for "Very Bad People" shortly after her niece used it to describe some bad guys in a shoot 'em up action movie. Somehow it dehumanized them, just using initials allowed Hedwick to make them an abstraction of evil and not people. She could not imagine a horrible mistake leading to the death of true innocents.

"I don't know what to say," Hedwick said.

This was the first sign of softness and compassion she had allowed to show since this mission had begun. There was a time she had been more of a tender person, but this job had suppressed that part of her. Now this man, who had suffered due to an accident, brought that human part of her back to the surface.

Michelle, of course, knew almost everything Tommy said. She had heard it before, during the time they had spent together, and from the police reports she read. That did not make it easier for her to hear it again.

"Please be honest with me. That thing, and that man in the pit changed everything. Lies and secrets are no longer business as usual. Did you kill Gregg or did he kill himself?" Tommy asked.

"Wait here," Hedwick said.

She stood and left the room. In a minute she returned holding a black and white composition notebook. Tommy immediately it as the same sort of notebook they had used in English class in high school. Hedwick opened the notebook to a bookmarked page, and handed it to Tommy. He began to read the tiny, precise hand writing.

I have spent a lot of time thinking about death since the accident. How is it that I am still alive? The police and Tommy and the doctors blame the medicine for what happened. I'm not so sure. Chemicals do not have conscience. Chemicals do not have consciousness. But that raises the question of what is our consciousness then? As humans we have consciousness and conscience and neurobiologists tell us that our mind is nothing more than an incredibly complex series of chemical reactions and interactions. At what point does the chemical that is a drug which affects our consciousness become itself part of our consciousness. And if it does become part of our consciousness how do we not ourselves become part of each other's consciousnesses, when we exchange chemicals with others. We breathe the same air as other people so when do we breathe in parts of their consciousness. Why can't we know their thoughts when we are in the same space and some of the molecules that leave them are breathed in to us. At what point does the complexity of ones consciousness begin and transfer of the chemicals of others. Does the compartment of the brain contain the consciousness? How does consciousness get defined then if...

It went on this way for a time. The intricate loops of false logic and speculation showing the depth of the psychosis that Gregg was usually able to conceal in his day to day interactions with the world. Then at the bottom of a page, Tommy read:

If I do kill myself and I use a gun I will do it with my right hand. If I can put even a tiny bit of doubt into someone's mind about whether I actually did it then perhaps, by their doubt, I might be remembered a bit better. If there is a question about whether or not I did it then they wouldn't think of me badly. That is one thing that has stopped me, I have lived for so long with this guilt and people know I killed others that I can't be seen as an ongoing killer. Drugs or not I do not want to be remembered for killing myself.

"He was dead when we got there," Hedwick said.

Tommy looked up from the journal.

"We figured out he had taken some pictures and we were going to try and get those from him, but he had killed himself by the time we got there to talk to him. Then we saw the footage from the school and figured out he had passed the phone to you," she said.

"So what would you have done if you caught us?" Michelle asked.

"Caught you?" Hedwick asked. Then she got a funny look on her face then looked almost a bit sad. She debated about whether or not to tell them the rest of it, but ultimately concluded Tommy had been right. There were no more secrets.

"We haven't been chasing you. We have been watching you. We saw you at the farm. We followed you to the root beer stand. We saw you get the phones at the convenience store. I did like what you did to get rid of the phone. I'll be telling that story for years."

Hedwick laughed. All three relaxed. Tommy had not realized how tense he had been until he had felt some of the tension ooze away. He was amazed at the power of laughter.

"We only wanted to be sure you wouldn't do something we might all regret with those pictures. Now I don't know what might be regretful and what might be right," she said.

"Why didn't you just come to us?" Tommy asked.

"Often in that type of encounter, we become perceived as the aggressor. Those we approach feel either they are victims or they become aggressive in return. We have found it works better to just observe, unless it is obvious that something bad is going to happen. Tonight you came to us, and we knew you were going to. Of course the way things did happen, we could not foresee. It's a whole new ballgame now," Hedwick said.

"So. What did you have planned before things took this left turn?" Tommy asked.

"We were going to try to play good cop and try and get those pictures from you. But that's all moot right now." She said.

"So who are you? This isn't regular Army. Why the cover story?" Michelle asked.

Tommy looked at Michelle and raised an eyebrow. The same question had passed through his mind several times, but he had not been ready to ask yet.

"I was waiting for that too," Hedwick said. "That, I'm afraid, is complicated."

Chapter 52

Sue found Robert in the office, asleep on the Naugahyde sofa. His face was in a small puddle of his own drool. There were ants swarming the remainder of a sandwich on a plate on the floor where Robert left it.

Sue smiled at the ants. She had instantly seen the analogy to their own situation. The ants had been going about their normal lives, day to day, very much the same. Then, as if from nowhere, there something incredible appeared. It was something beyond the ants' comprehension and previous experience. Yet like the ants there was, despite a lack of understanding, all the evidence of their senses telling them the impossible was right there in front of them.

Sue hesitated. She wondered how long Robert had been asleep. The other three had been talking in the break room. She had not disturbed them. Jonathan had said she was to send Robert next. Her mind was so loaded with all the details of their dialogue, and all the new ideas the conversation had generated, that she could not question what had seemed like a direct order. Besides, she wanted to go begin writing some of the ideas down while there were still fresh in her mind.

"Robert," she said.

He did not stir. Sue was instantly worried. The few times she had woken him in the past, he had been alert and upright before the last of the sound had stopped reverberating. This deep sleep was unusual. For a moment she had a thought that he may have had a stroke or been drugged.

"Robert," she said, louder than the first time.

This time an eye opened. It stared straight ahead roughly at the chair to Sue's left. She was afraid once again that he had blown a gasket. Then he sat up slowly. He blinked then looked at Sue. He reached up and wiped the spittle from his cheek.

He smacked his lips. Sue was reminded of her sister's pug, who did almost exactly the same thing when he woke. Two images juxtaposed themselves in her mind and she had to bite the inside of her cheek to stifle a laugh. She saw in her mind a man with a pug face carrying a pug dog with Robert's face. Normally such things would not come to mind at all. If they did, they would not be funny. But for some reason—perhaps sheer exhaustion—she found this image highly humorous

"So what do you know?" Robert asked. This was not a conversation starter or a casual question. This was an order for information.

Sue felt better. She knew that after his brief pause to reboot, Robert's brain was back on track.

"I know that the technology out there is so advanced it is beyond me in several areas. I also know that I am going to somehow be responsible for the development of that technology. I know that all of us have a role to play in what comes next, as far as the big picture. I know that you are next up to talk to the man in the pit. The recorders are still all going on BARRy, so don't try to remember everything. Instead focus on trying to grasp the big picture," Sue said.

"Alright. Nothing for it I guess," Robert said.

He stood, took a moment to stretch his hands toward the ceiling, then without a word left the room.

Sue waited a moment then followed. She went to the small room at the end of the hall where some cots had been set up. She sat down on the one furthest from the door. She took off her shoes and socks. Something about seeing her feet reminded her of the story of Paul when the scales fell from his eyes.

She had always been happy with her body. The exception was her feet. She perpetually had calluses due to her habit of buying the same shoes that did not fit particularly well. She had, at last count, nine pairs of the same canvas high tops. She had started wearing them in high school, when she had needed to buy her own shoes. She bought them then because they were cheap. Now she wore them as a statement about not conforming to expectations. Years ago she had gone to the store with the intent to buy herself some expensive, sexy shoes. She left with another pair of canvas high tops. That moment had crystallized her determination to be her own person.

She lay down on the cot and closed her eyes. She was exhausted, but did not expect to sleep. She pondered the problem of William. She knew he was smart, perhaps second only to herself in the group in brute intelligence. She also knew he had never really let on just how smart he was. It had only been in the sometimes amazing solutions to some very tricky problems she had gotten a clue to the true depth of William's mind. She was intrigued.

It was about the same time she had realized William's genius that she and Robert had also realized William had been covertly gathering information. The reason for this had remained a mystery until a few minutes ago.

"What will we do about him? Do we need to do anything? Direct confrontation or subversive management to deal with this?" These questions swirled about in her head until, without realizing it, she fell into her own black hole of sleep.

Chapter 53

"So, what are you? Black ops? Majestic? From Area 51?" Tommy said with a smile?

During his days in the Army, he had heard rumors of rumors about some of the covert things that went on under the radar. Of course there were the Rangers, the Seals and the Green Berets. They all undertook the occasional operation that would not be considered the normal course of national policy, but met objectives for which there were no other means of achievement. Tommy knew there were operations that would never be known even to the small minority of the military leadership.

"We are…unofficial, but loosely part of the military. There are about 1.5 million soldiers and another 1.5 million reserves, with about a quarter of a million officers in the entire U.S. military. In any organization that size there are holes, places where accountability is not, and cannot, always be strictly monitored. We exist in those holes," Hedwick said.

"But what keeps the 'official' Army out of here?" Michelle asked.

"Two things. First, this is a backwoods, small time operation as far as anyone not in the know is aware. They have no intention of coming out here once they know it is being handled. And they don't care who is handling it or how they handle it as long as it is not their problem. Second, they haven't gotten orders to come out here. Simply put, no one else cares," Hedwick said.

"Limited budget and understaffing leading to apathy." Tommy said.

"That sounds like a recipe for successful secrecy," Michelle said.

"It has worked very well. Robert, who is in command here, has become a master of keeping secrets, right under peoples' noses. He is able to get what is needed to do a job and at the same time keep it all under the radar."

"Why not tell the truth about what is in that pit?" Michelle asked, her journalistic sensibility taking over.

"Part of that is orders. Those up the chain of command distinctly told us not to. The other part is that we really didn't know what we were dealing with when the time came to make a statement." Hedwick said.

"I really think we need to get some rest. We don't know how much we will get in the next few days," Tommy said, cutting the conversation short. He wanted to talk to Michelle alone. "And beside I haven't gotten much sleep the past few days either."

"I think that is a good idea," Hedwick agreed. She recognized it for what it was and was fine with being left alone. She had some things to think about, and would do better in contemplation by herself.

"There are a couple different places we have set up bunks, or you are free to take any of the unused office spaces you would like," Hedwick said. "They are just down the hall to the left."

"Thanks," Tommy said.

"Will you wake us if anything changes?" Michelle asked.

"I will."

In her own mind, Hedwick was not so sure she would. She was still not so comfortable with these two. She kept trying to figure out what they were up to. Why were they here? She understood how they had gotten involved, but was not sure of their purpose in the bigger picture.

She watched as they went down the hallway and tuned into one of the small offices to the left. She waited for the door to close then headed outside to think. She was always able to think more clearly when she was outside. For her, there was something about being inside that made her feel trapped. She was not claustrophobic. In fact she had been in many narrow and cramped places without a hint of panic. She just did not feel at her best inside. She had serous thinking to do, and outside was the place for it.

Tommy and Michelle closed the door to the small office. It was dimly lit by a single bulb lamp on the desk. The lamp had a green, half cylinder shade that was exactly like the one that had been on Tommy's grandmother's piano when he had been a child—at least until he broke it roughhousing with his cousins during the annual Christmas party. The desk was a cheap Formica topped metal behemoth like his elementary school teachers sat behind.

"What do you think?" Michelle asked.

"About what?" Tommy asked back.

"Do you really think there is this group that operates in the holes, like she says? That sounds so much like something you would see in a movie," she said.

"I guess I do. When I was in the Army, there were rumors of this sort of thing. Most of it I put down to just talk. There was one time, right before I was discharged, that really got my attention. I was on base walking between the mess and the PX when an all black hummer and two camo Hummers drove up to the CO's office. There were no plates or ID numbers on any of the vehicles and the soldiers I saw didn't have any unit insignias on their uniforms. That was strange. Just like those guys out at the road block didn't have any insignias either. I suppose it is possible," Tommy said.

"Yeah, I guess. My question is whether or not we are going to get out of this alive, and, if so, in what condition." Her voice was full of weary anxiety.

"I feel like our future is a trap. It is already set for us and we didn't have a choice about stepping into it. But it is not other than the cause of events that are going to happen. We don't know what those events are going to be any more than we did before all of this started. Knowing that they will happen doesn't mean we will know what they are before they happen."

"Ugh. I'm too tired to think straight about that sort of thing. I'm going to try and sleep," Michelle said.

"Before you do, would you answer one more question?" he asked. This was the real reason he had wanted to talk to her. The idea bouncing around in his head had come to a crux and he wanted to know if he was crazy or not.

"Okay," Michelle said.

"I've been thinking, and I think I would like to get to know you better. I know this sounds like I'm sixteen, but would you like to go out with me when this whole thing is over? If we live through it, I mean." He asked.

"I...I hadn't really thought about that. What brought this up?" Michelle said.

In reality she had thought about getting together with Tommy for some time. When she had first known him during the months after his wife and daughter's deaths, she had first thought about it. She had felt so sorry for him. Seeing his pain, she wanted desperately to help him get over it. She wanted to help him recover, to somehow try to help him to mend the broken places that his wife and daughter's deaths had left deep within him.

Michelle had always been a fixer. She had always been the one to whom her girlfriends would come for advice and solace when their boyfriends acted the jerk. She enjoyed that role and filled it well. Anytime she saw someone suffering, she wanted to fix the problem, to make things better. Her inability to fix everything for everyone had been her torment. She had been forced to learn not to burden herself as much with situations beyond her ability to control. She had learned to accept her limitations in that regard. It did not, however, eliminate her desire to help in any. It simply helped her feel a little better when she wasn't able to take away someone's suffering.

The few times she and Tommy had gone out quickly revealed to Michelle there would be no relationship beyond friendship, at least at that point in Tommy's life. So she had gone on with hers, focusing on her writing. She moved on. The thought of helping him, though, had never really faded. Now he was the one opening up the subject of their being together. She was confused and excited.

"For a while now, maybe a year or so, the loneliness I felt after the accident has started to change," Tommy said. At first it was a loneliness for my wife and daughter. I missed them and felt like the only way I wouldn't feel lonely was to have them back. But now that loneliness, even though I still miss them terribly, is...more just the loneliness of being alone. Does that make any sense?"

"It does," she answered.

"You have been one of the nicest people to me through all of this. It seemed like you knew I needed to be by myself for a while. But now I'm ready to not be alone any more. I would like for us to give it a chance and see where things end up," Tommy said.

"I'd like that. I can't imagine what you had to go though but..." Michelle said.

"I don't want you to," Tommy said.

Michelle yawned despite herself.

"It looks like you need some rest."

"I think so. Try to get some rest yourself," she said.

They both lay down on cots. Despite her desire and need to

sleep, Michelle wasn't able to drift off. For his part, Tommy felt a great relief in telling Michelle his thoughts, and fell asleep quickly.

Chapter 54

Robert left the office feeling slightly groggy. Something was not right with him lately. He should be wide awake. He looked at his watch and was surprised to see he had been asleep for nearly three hours. He should be refreshed and alert after that much time. He finally decided he did not want to get any older.

In the cafeteria he found that the others had departed. He could hear no voices. Perhaps they had gone to rest. Robert really didn't care. He just needed caffeine. The soda machine had been unlocked since the last time he had been in here. He grabbed an energy drink and a bottle of water.

There was a small mirror next to the hand sink in the corner of the room where Robert caught a glimpse of himself. He was shocked by his appearance. Slowly he walked to the mirror. How haggard he looked. Then it hit him. It was Hedwick. Everything that had happened between them, he had managed to put in a compartment locked deep within his mind. Now, with her here, all of it was seeping up through the cracks, like radon in his psyche. His concern for her, he realized, could destroy him. And he knew the suppression of his feelings for Hedwick, and all that had happened, was no longer going to work. He would have to deal with this, and sooner than later. One more time, he pushed away his feelings. This was not the time to deal with it. There were more important things requiring his immediate attention.

He turned to the sink and splashed his face with cold water. Looking in the mirror again, he shook his head. He chugged the energy drink, went to the fridge for a second bottle of water and headed out to the pit.

The air was still heavy and thick with humidity, but starting to get cooler. The heat that had been absorbed by the rock all around him during the day was now radiating back. Robert could see condensation beginning to form on the windshields of the few vehicles in the lot. Despite the warmth, Robert still felt a chill as he stepped outside. It had nothing to do with temperature. His nerves were making him shiver.

Robert walked into the pit and paused at the cage. He wanted to grab a pad of paper and something to write with. Although everything would be recorded and could be reviewed at a later time, he had discovered long before that he thought better when he could write things down as they occurred to him. There was a mechanism in his mind that allowed him, when he wrote, to see connections he was not otherwise able to grasp when simply listening to someone. Perhaps it was the integration of multiple pathways in his brain—pathways for listening, physical movement and both hearing language and the abstraction of writing language—that increased his processing ability. He had known for a long time of this trick for finding connections. It was something he had first discovered it in high school when he realized that his class notes often had connections written that had not been mentioned in class by his teachers. It had served him well in the past. The funny thing was, he almost never had to refer back to what he had written. It was the process of writing itself that allowed for deeper insights requiring no post facto analysis. On the few occasions he had gone back to his notes, they had been almost incomprehensible. For him, it was the process, not the product, that produced the results.

Robert left the cage with a yellow legal pad and the stub of a pencil. The pencil had seemed out of place in the cage with all of Sue's high tech gadgets. Then he remembered Sue never wrote in ink. She had told him why once, but the exact reason had slipped his mind. He was trying to remember it as he rounded the corner of the rock wall.

Robert's mind was immediately seized by the present. He was taken back again by the size of the object. The man in the white clothes waited for him.

"Come, Robert. Let us talk about what your role is going to be," Jonathan said.

Robert walked to Jonathan and sat on the rock where he sat before. He waited. Robert rarely started a conversation unless he was in a position of power. Though he did not feel threatened, but was unsure of his position in this situation. He was not sure really what this situation was. He would wait and try to get a read on things based on what the man said.

The moment before the silence and the staring of the "man in white", as Robert thought of him, became uncomfortable Jonathan spoke.

"You are here because you have a role to play. It is not a role you expect or a role you have been prepared for. But it is your role and you will perform it perfectly."

"And what would that role be?" Robert asked.

Chapter 55

Robert waited for Jonathan to explain what he was expected to do. Jonathan looked at him, then took a deep breath.

"Your role will be more dangerous than you might think. It is also perhaps the most essential in all of this. You have to tell the truth about what is going on here," he said.

Robert was dumbfounded. He sucked in a deep breath. His mind began to reel. He had spent his last fifteen years living in a world of deception and half-truth. He had perpetuated the majority of misinformation himself. Often his rationale had been that the truth would cause more harm than good. Sometimes that was truth. Sometimes it was not. Often, deception was simply the more expedient option. Sometime deception was in Robert's self interest.

The idea of actually telling the truth astounded and deeply troubled Robert. He was uneasiness for several reasons. First, to say the least, his superiors would not be happy. Telling the truth would almost surely cost him his career. Possibly his life.

Second, a lie was already in place, vested by yesterday's press conference. To recant the story now would cause a domino effect. There would be questions about which story was correct. There would be questions about why there had been deception in the first place. Questions would arise about who Robert really was and for whom he actually worked. In the long run the biggest questions would be about other stories set forth by official channels; were they also deceptions?

The third reason would be the worst for Robert himself. If he told the truth about this, he knew he would have to examine his past actions and what damage they might have caused. He had been a master of forgetting his own deceit when the outcome matched what was expected of him. He knew if he had to tell the truth now, he would begin to look at all of those things and very likely he would not like what he saw. Deception had been a way of life. To tell the truth now would force a reevaluation of his life.

"How much of the truth do I tell?" Robert asked.

"Everything. You will need to tell not only the truth, but you will expose that what you had originally told the press had been a lie, sanctioned by your superiors, to prevent the truth from coming out," Jonathan said.

Robert paused. Then slowly he said, "You know that may get me killed? Why would I do that? I'm not saying I won't, but I need a very good reason."

"I understand. I don't ask this lightly, but it's what's best. Your telling the truth will start a cascade leading to much of what will be necessary," Jonathan said.

"I'm afraid," Robert admitted.

Fear, like the truth, was something that Robert had ignored for a long time. He had been in situations in which he felt fear. He had been able to push it down, ignore it, to get the job done. That distraction of the needing to do his job, and the necessary overriding of his own emotion, was disarmed by the completely new idea of being honest and forthright.

The last time he felt fear like this—the fear of impending consequences from doing the right thing, and not been able to suppress them—was when he was nineteen and in college. He had been cornered by a group of thugs. Walking back to his dorm from the bar where he had been drinking, he made an "impaired" decision and cut through the alley of a bad neighborhood. During the day it was a safe place. At night it was not. This happened before the time when he had learned to always be aware of his surroundings. He had been cornered by five men who intended to rob him. His fear had energized him. The fight or flight reaction had given him energy to flee. He zipped up a fire escape so quickly the thugs had not tried to follow him.

That event also started him on the first steps of the path that led to where he was now. That fear had caused him to begin studying karate. The combination of his university courses and his rapid progress and natural talent for the martial arts brought him to the attention of those who eventually recruited him into his present position. The fear of that event had created a turning point in his life. He understood the fear of what he was being asked to do now would surely precipitate another change in the course of his life.

"Fear, like many reactions, has a purpose. But how you respond to fear is what is important. Fear is often a reaction to a perceived threat, not a real one. Your fear is such. Let me assure you, even though bringing out the truth will not be easy, your eventual satisfaction with the results will more than compensate for any discomfort. That is as much as I can tell you," Jonathan said. "The logical argument for you to come forward with the truth is a bit more complicated. If you believe me, then my simply telling you will be sufficient. If not, then there are other arguments, deeper arguments I can use to convince you."

Robert paused. His brain simply overwhelmed. He had not considered any of this as a question of belief. The idea of his future in the balance, based on belief and not hard evidence, bothered him. It rang too much like the spiritual arguments he struggled with as a teenager. He had, as a teen, simply decided to delay making any decisions about faith, eternity and whether there was a God. While the context was different, the difficulty of trusting in something, believing in it simply because it needed to believed in, came rushing to the surface.

Then it hit him. He already had allowed that kind of faith into his life. Blind trust had been given to Robert's faith in the capabilities of Sue and Hedwick and in the other men and women he worked with. He believed they would have his back in any situation, regardless of the danger to themselves. He believed what Sue told him, even though he knew he would not be able to understand a detailed explanation. Sue believed what this man said. Therefore, Robert decided to take the biggest leap of faith he could remember.

"I believe you. What do I do next?" Robert asked.

"There are two things. The first is that you and Sue must decide what to do about William James. I know you are aware of his information gathering. He wants to expose the whole hidden operations segment of the intelligence business. He has enough information to do just that. Of course you will deflate his balloon by what the second thing I will request. I have already talked to Sue about William. You and she need to decide how you will handle this. So the first thing you will do is talk to her about that decision.

"Keep in mind that William is extremely intelligent and has enough information to destroy not only this operation, but to also raise questions about the entire intelligence community. Going forward he can be either a friend or enemy. I won't tell you what to do, but you will need to decide how you two will handle him before you deal with the second thing.

"Second. In the morning you will release a statement and explain everything. Michelle, the woman who was brought in from the tunnel, will help you. She is a reporter. She will help you craft and distribute your statement. After that, the object and I will be gone, and things will move quickly. Just remember to go with your gut and it will all be fine. I am here as evidence of that. I think that is all I need to tell you. Go and discuss with Sue how to handle William. Before you do, please tell Hedwick to come see me next," Jonathan said.

Robert, lost in his own thoughts, and headed back to the office building. He wanted another drink. There were other things, though, that had to be done.

Chapter 56

The humidity hit Hedwick as she left the air conditioning. The earlier rain and the heat absorbed by the rock beneath her feet during the day made it feel like a sauna. Still she was glad to be outside, able to breathe real unprocessed, unfiltered air.

As she stepped through the door she was struck by a memory of a night like this one, many years before. She had crawled out of her bedroom window onto the roof of her parents' house. The air was humid, like this tonight. The heat radiating from the shingles was very much like the heat rising from the massive heat sink of the limestone under her feet.

Thinking her parents had gone to sleep, she had snuck out to have a cigarette. She had started smoking, due to peer pressure, when she was sixteen and found it very hard to quit, even when she no longer considered smoking to be cool.

That was the night she had gotten caught by her father. He had gotten up to get a drink and saw her on the roof from the bathroom window. Instead of yelling or getting upset, he crawled out and sat beside her. They had talked about her growing up and how he was proud of her. He told her he did not approve of her smoking, but said it in a calm voice. Once said, that was the end of it. He went on to talk about other things. They sat on the roof almost all night. That night she was no longer "Daddy's little girl". Both of them realized she had started down the path to being a strong woman. Ironically, he had been so proud of her.

Hedwick had not smoked for more than five years. She had smoked her last on the night of her father's funeral. Now, she really wanted a cigarette. It was funny that the only time she craved one was when she thought of her father.

She shook herself. There were more immediate things to think about. She needed to try and figure out what was happening and what she should do about it.

So much of the world was far beyond what most people saw. A

great deal of what happened in the daily life of most people was exactly as it appeared. There were other realities, though, beyond what most people ever experienced that would shake up society were they to become known. This thing in the pit was one of those things. The incident in Arizona was another. Her job was, in great measure, to keep such things hidden.

Occasionally, part of her job was to plant misinformation, to create events that never happened. If the right misinformation was leaked, it would draw conspiracy theorists like moths to a porch light, distracting them from what was actually going on. One of the easiest ways to do this was leaking information about the Kennedy assassination, grey information in the form of mountains of documents. Another, her favorite, was to generate lots of documents about UFOs that had been redacted in the most tantalizing ways, without really giving away any new information. Perhaps the most effective, however, was to publish scientific research papers that hinted about secret or otherworldly technology, without sufficient detail to prove the technology had been developed from existing technology, and not reverse engineered from other sources.

This was different. This situation was unique. Usually there was the object within an operation that needed to be protected—or eliminated—and kept from the public. However this man, in this thing, had his own agenda. And, if she understood correctly, that agenda had already been fulfilled. Ultimately there was nothing she could do about it.

The feeling of helplessness frustrated her. It was not fear. It was the same feeling she had when she had been unable to convince her eighth grade teacher that you can not make assumptions in a logic problem. The teacher based her entire argument for the solution of the problem on the assumption that most individuals acted in a certain way, an assumption not stated in the problem. Hedwick had argued her point clearly. The teacher even said that technically it was right, but still had not given Hedwick credit for a correct answer. It was at that point she had come to the decision that she would not allow others to arbitrarily dictate to her without her taking some action. She had gone to the principal to complain. He had wimped out and said it was not his place to change grades. She had gotten a letter from a professor of logic at the local university putting forth the same argument, stating the incorrectness of the teacher's conclusion. She took it to the school board and even sent it to the company who had originally published the worksheet from which the logic problem came. The teacher had relented at last when Hedwick mentioned writing a letter to the local paper.

After that, Hedwick had not allowed herself to be victim to any unfair circumstances, at least not without retaliation. This seemed to be just such a circumstance, only one in which she had no recourse. Up to this point she had either gone to whatever lengths were necessary to reverse or correct an unfair circumstance. Or she had, on the few rare occasions when that had not worked, gotten revenge. As she liked to think of it, "dispensed justice as it truly should be, not as the system said it should be". She was not always proud of those moments, but neither did she regret them.

This situation was driving her crazy. There were too many variables. It was not so much the number of variables, as that she had no control over them. What could she do that would not cause her to go completely mad? The dichotomy of fate and freewill had always been a mindbender for her. It was why she had rejected the idea of a God who knew all and saw all, but made original sin and salvation a choice. It did not seem fair to her. She made, at that point, a conscious decision to forget this line of thought. She would ask those questions of the man in the pit. Her own speculation was not getting her anywhere.

There were other, more pressing, things to consider. She knew she needed to think about an exit plan. That had always been her role. She had always been the safety net of every operation. It had gone badly in Arizona. It had been her fault. She simply had to accept that. Now, she thought, this may be a "no exit" situation.

Despite her need to figure these things out, Hedwick's mind continually wandered. She kept wishing she knew in advance what she was going to be doing. If it was already known, would knowing it herself make it possible to change any of it? The thought came to her that, if she changed something as a result of her knowledge of the future, it might prevent the arrival of man from the future with whom they were speaking in the pit. If so, would that not negate her knowledge of the future, and therefore make it impossible for her to change—thereby resulting in the future happening just as it would to result in the thing appearing in the pit. It was a vicious cycle of cause: fate and effect from which Hedwick could not escape. She was running the cycle through for about the twentieth time, when she heard feet on the gravel.

"It is your turn," said Robert.

Chapter 57

Robert walked back into the building. He headed to the cafeteria. He got another bottle of water from the refrigerator, and sat down at one of the tables.

He began to mull over what Jonathan had told him. Dealing with William would be simple enough. As Robert saw it, there were two possible choices. The first was to include William in what was going to be happening in the morning. The second was to confront him and send him away.

The first was to Robert the far more attractive option. It would be so much easier to keep him under control if William believed his own agenda was being met. The information that would be released would remain controlled. The second option left too many loose ends. Robert and Sue had not been able to form a complete picture of what William knew and what he could prove. If they could keep William on their side, keeping truly damaging information form the public would be much easier.

At this point, though, Robert was unsure of what constituted safe information to release and what constituted damaging information.

The idea of telling the truth about this situation indeed frightened him. At the same time, it was exciting in a way that he would not have anticipated. For many years he had lived a life in the shadows, not telling the truth about much of anything. Lying had been a way of life.

He had even been lying to himself for a long time. He had known it in the back of his mind, but had not put words to it. Lately he had been lying to himself, denying he had lost some of his edge and his focus. He knew that he had moments when his mind wandered. He had always been able to find excuses and pretend they were valid. He had been lying to himself that it was because he was tired. He had lied to himself that it was because of being overworked, with too many responsibilities.

He knew it was something else. He knew it was that he was quite simply done. He was done with the life of not existing. He was done with the life of not really living. He was done with the life without a place. The anonymity and the restlessness had worn on him. When he had first started, he loved it. This life fit with his desire to have no roots. But he no longer felt it was what he wanted. He had denied this to himself for a long time, mostly because he had not been able to figure a way out.

He had already exceeded the average life expectancy of people in his position by several years. He had been in positions where he could have died more than once. Those times had not bothered him. In Arizona, on the operation that had fallen apart, he had realized he loved Hedwick on the same day she had almost died. But, even then—faced with the desperation of nearly losing her, he had not seen a way out.

Here at last was his way out. Telling the truth was something he had never considered. As he thought about it, it made perfect sense. Of course it was fantastically risky. If he did not go about it the right way, it might well cost him his life. Perhaps that would be the place where William would be of the greatest use. Robert suddenly realized that if William had been gathering this information, he certainly had a plan to keep safe after it was released. William obviously had a cause, but did not impress Robert as one who wished to go the path of a martyr. The thought that there might be a way out excited him. He knew that if he managed to survive the initial few days, his knowledge of how to live in the shadows, and his connections who owed him their own lives could keep him safe for a long time.

Robert realized he had lost track of what the truth really was. His grandmother had always interpreted truth, and honesty and faith as the essential goods. She had also considered trust in others as a prime virtue. As a young man, Robert had held a similar faith in the basic goodness of those things. He had respected his grandmother and her faith in God. Deception, lying and many of the other things that had become the everyday way of life for Robert, were things that she would have found abhorrent were she still alive. He knew he had turned away from the virtues she had instilled in him growing up. The exact way that had happened was complex. But Robert felt he would have enough time to sort that out. Perhaps, he might even use this as a first step in trying to recover a faith like that of his grandmother.

Robert wondered what his grandmother might say. He could almost hear her saying "Why are you afraid of the truth. If telling the truth was commanded by God, what makes you think you are the exception to that?"

Robert reflected on the question. He had gone to church. He had witnessed the faith of many of the people. It was something he had admired in them. It was not something he had ever really fully understood or come to possess himself. Now, perhaps he might be able to look at this part of his life in more detail. He agreed with Asimov's statement that "technology, sufficiently advanced is indistinguishable from magic." Despite this, he had seen things that really made him question whether there was something more than the objective universe.

What was the truth? What did truth really mean? Not the facts, for he knew the true facts and the lies and cover-up stories backwards and forwards. He wanted to try and wrap his mind around what truth really meant. Was there even any truth beyond what perception tells us? Robert thought about Stephen King's "The Langoliers" in which the past of reality was devoured into nothingness and each minute was a new creation. Then he thought about the discussions he had with Sue about quantum mechanics and how observation was what actually determined reality. Robert did not understand it, but got the impression from Sue that reality as we know it, truth in fact, does not exist outside what we observe.

For Robert, the truth was something that one simply knows. Truth is reality. For Robert, what his senses told him and what his logical mind could deduce was truth. Even though Robert had been spinning and twisting the truth for years in the service of his mission goals, when he really thought about it, it all kept coming back to the essential point. He really did know truth.

He rose. It was time to talk to Sue, to decide if his decision to include William was in line with her thoughts. He knew if she thought there was a better course of action, she was probably right. He realized this was another example of faith. He would go with what she thought was right. He walked out of the cafeteria and started down the hallway to find her

Chapter 58

Hedwick walked toward the pit. As she did, she began to shift her thoughts to the men who had died at the beginning of this whole event. Her human side began to express itself. How could someone, who obviously knew the past results of his actions, do something that he knew would result in the death of other human beings?

She realized then she would not be asking these questions if she had been in charge of the project that resulted in those men's deaths. She realized the reality of the event occurring at all made their deaths inevitable. Those deaths were part of this event. The event occurred in the present and in the future. If the deaths had been attempted to be avoided by some effort of someone in the future, none of this would have happened and she would not be here.

So the best that Hedwick could figure was that the death of those men was going to happen, whether it was from the arrival of this object or some other factor. She had always believed in the idea that each individual was going to live certain amount of time and then die. She had seen too many instances of people who should have died, but did not. Her mother had more than once said, "It wasn't their time."

She had also ,more than once, seen people who had died as a result of being in the wrong place at the wrong time. She knew it was a cliché, but it held true. As she thought about it, she realized that was what happened to those men. She had never thought too much about the bigger picture behind this. If asked, she would not be able to express it as anything other than fate. She had tried not to think too much about what holding this sort of belief really meant in the broader sense of what belief in anything really meant.

The part she still had trouble with, after these mind exercises, was the man who had killed himself. She had never been able to find a good reconciliation between suicide and the idea of fate. Suicide always seemed a wildcard in the cosmic game of fate.

It was not that she did not understand the desperation that would lead someone to end their own life. She had felt on more than one occasion that suicide was at least on the table as an option for her. She had never considered it seriously or made any plans toward that end. Still, she could understand how a person could be so hopeless and desperate as to kill himself.

The part that left her spinning her wheels: was it was "the time" of the person who committed suicide when they pulled the trigger, took the overdose or drove their car off a bridge? Was it "their time", or by their actions were they throwing a wrench into the cosmic timeline. Or was the idea of this sort of fate just actually another example of the human brain trying to find a handle on something that is inherently chaotic?

As she walked past the cage, she snapped out of her reflection. She began to think ahead about what was really going on here. She began to wonder what the next hour, the next day and the next week would bring. She had trained herself to think in blocks of time. For her it was dealing with the immediate, the pressing and the long term. She knew a week was, for most professionals, more likely to be considered immediate than long term. For Hedwick, a week ahead was often almost impossible to predict. Most of the time she felt lucky if her intended plans held together for twenty-four hours.

For now, she was focused on the next few minutes. What could she find out from this mystery man? What was the big picture of why he was here? Was what he had told them earlier the truth, or just convenient cover? Was time travel really the mechanism of how he was here, or was there something else going on?

These questions buzzed around in her head as she went around the corner. She saw the man waiting for her. The calm with which he waited unnerved her. She paused for a moment, then walked on in her best power walk. She hoped that the fact she was projecting self-confidence would not betray her underlying uncertainty about what even the next few minutes would bring.

When she got within earshot Jonathan said in a loud but gentle voice, "Hedwick, you are the hardest one to talk to here. Your doubts will make this difficult. But let me assure you that you need to do nothing but follow your instincts. If you do that things will work out the way they are supposed to. The fact that we are talking to each other is evidence that it does."

"Yeah, about that. That is what you keep saying, but I'm not sure

I entirely buy it. Your logic makes sense, but why should I accept that as the only explanation?" Hedwick asked. Her voice was flat, no hint of emotion, either positive or negative.

"Very good. Your doubts will serve you well. But let me answer your question with a question or two of my own. Do you see this object?" Jonathan asked, sweeping his hand toward the giant curve of the object.

"Yes."

"And you believe I am here talking to you?"

"Yes."

"And what makes you believe these things?"

"I see that thing. I see and can hear you," Hedwick said.

"By the evidence of your senses, you believe. Take the following evidence, and believe what you will."

Jonathan held out his hand. A newspaper appeared with the next day's date and the headline of Time Traveler Appears in Midwest. There was a picture of Robert at a podium with the reporter and Sue standing to one side.

Hedwick rushed forward and tried to grab the paper. She could not touch it. As her fingers touched the place where the paper should have been, she felt a slight tingle which reminded her of licking a nine volt battery. She looked up into the eyes of Jonathan.

"This is a projection. I am a projection and that object is a projection. This projection is from the future. If you are ready, I will tell you what your role will be."

Chapter 59

As Michelle lay awake, she could hear Tommy's breathing get slower and shallower, then become a light snoring. She wondered at his ability to fall asleep in almost any situation. She thought about the situation they were in. She had a million questions she wanted to ask. She spent the time trying to get her thoughts in order to ask the most important questions first. Her training as a journalist had included that as an essential law. Ask the big questions first. Put the most important information at the beginning of the article.

As she sorted these questions, another thought kept popping up in her mind. She realized everything that was happening, these very moments, were of profound historical import. The reality of practical time travel would cause such an upheaval in society that it would create an incredible shift in the collective consciousness. That was of course if anyone believed it. There was always resistance to something so profound.

As she was thinking about the change this would have on so many levels, she began to overlay the idea of having a relationship with Tommy. Michelle realized that not just the big picture, but her own personal picture could be changing. She started to drift off to sleep. She dreamed she was standing at the edge of the quarry pit. She looked into the pit, but could not see the bottom. She fell forward. She fell with a feeling of being totally out of control. Just before she hit bottom, she jerked awake. Her heart pounded. She sat up and looked over to where Tommy continued to snore softly. She knew she was safe, but not for how long.

Despite the enormity of everything happening around her. Despite her thoughts of what the future would hold for the world, she started to think again about Tommy. She began to wonder if it could work between them. For some unknown reason, a quote from a movie came to mind. "Relationships that start during intense situations, never last." Or something to that effect. She wondered if that was really true. If it was, did it apply to her relationship with

Tommy? After all, she had known him for a long time. Would things change so much once the truth of what was going on surfaced—for she knew one way or another the truth had to get out, whether or not the people in charge helped her do it—that any kind of personal relationship would be impossible?

The other part of the equation was whether or not she could be the woman Tommy would need her to be. She had ended more than one relationship when it had become obvious that she could not be what the men she had been with had wanted. Through her entire adult life she had wrestled with self-esteem issues caused by trying to live up to the unrealistic expectations she placed on herself. Often it had been because it was what she thought those men wanted her to be. Those relationships, after the fact, made her take a look at herself. That introspection, along with some helpful therapy, helped her decide she only needed to satisfy one person—herself.

She had not dated much or had a serious relationship for several years. The last man she had dated was a chiropractor who kept making inappropriate, and childish, jokes about bones and adjustments. Three dates and out. She simply could not face listening to the innuendo any more. Before that, she had dated a plumber who had refused to see anything funny when she had made jokes about plumbing. These were just the last two examples in a string of men who were either letches or sticks in the mud. She had given up on finding someone who was a happy medium.

Now here was Tommy. She felt he was different from the first time she had met him. There was something intangible about him she had attributed to the trauma he had experienced. Everyone she had ever known who had gone through such a profound tragedy had a certain something about them she connected with, something she had never been able to put a finger on. She had never liked the idea of a person having an aura, as her hippie cousin had tried to explain it. But tragedy and trauma changed people in a perceptible way. Michelle had seen it more than once. The gentle part of Michelle wanted to comfort it. She wanted to fix the broken places in those people's lives.

She wondered if that was the only reason she was attracted to Tommy. Was her inner need to comfort the suffering, her desire to fix problems, making Tommy seem attractive? He certainly had pain. He had lived, intact, through something that had broken lesser men, and had survived and thrived. He was changed, but he had grown in so many ways.

At that moment she contemplated her need to fix Tommy, her mind performed one of those strange side that make no sense, except at the moment they happen. In a flash of insight, she thought that Tommy actually would be the one who would help her, would fix her. She knew it with certainty. She did not know what it was that he would be fixing, but she knew it to be true.

She found herself walking down the hallway toward the outside door. She hoped some fresh air and a look at the sky would help her clear her mind.

Chapter 60

Sue woke with a start. She had been dreaming about her college days. The dream began in a giant lecture hall full of students. She was sitting at the front of a physics class and taking notes. The professor said something that was not accurate and had just recently been refuted in a prominent journal. She called out to the professor that he was wrong and cited the article.

The professor looked at her strangely.

"Yes, I read that article. Although the math works and the results appear correct, I do not wish to believe it. Therefore, it must not be true." He said.

Sue was aghast. She argued with the professor.

"You are a scientist. How can you believe something that has been proven false? It's not like the concept of God, which simply has not yet been scientifically determined to be true or false. This has been proven false," she said.

"I fail to see the difference. Proof is only proof if we chose to believe it. If I don't accept the proof, then the conclusions don't matter."

Sue screamed in her dream. The professor's faulty logic was making her angry. It would have been a Taser moment had it happened in real life. The real situation had occurred differently. She had pointed out the professor's error and he had admitted he had not yet read the article. He stated he would suspend the class's current discussion until he had done so.

He had asked Sue to come to his office after class and discuss it. She had gone. They had spent almost three hours going through the article together. It had been one of her favorite memories from college. This dream had altered it into a nightmare.

It took Sue a moment to figure out where she was. The room was dark. It all came back. She began to wonder if Robert was back from the pit. She knew what they needed to do about William.

She sat up and pulled on her socks and shoes. This time she

stuck out her tongue at her own feet. She listened for a moment to determine if there was anyone near. She heard no one.

She stood and stretched then walked out the door.

She saw Robert just coming out of the cafeteria area. She had a moment to look at him before he saw her. He looked tired. That was not a surprise. What surprised Sue was the droop in his shoulders, and the pensiveness in Robert's face.

"Robert."

Robert looked up and smiled. The tiredness fell away and he looked like himself. There was something different in his smile, a peace that Sue had never seen. She had seen him smile before, but nothing like this. It made her smile in response.

"We need to talk about William," he said.

Robert walked down the hall and went into the little office where he had been sleeping when Sue had come to him. He gestured to Sue to join him in the room and closed the door behind her.

"What did he say to you?" Sue asked.

She was, typically, quite good at keeping her curiosity in check when they were in the midst of an operation. This time she could not contain her curiosity. Robert raised an eyebrow, something else she had never seen him do.

"I am to tell the truth," he said.

He looked at her. It was her turn to raise and eyebrow.

"About what?"

"About everything. I'm supposed to spill all the secrets of this place. Where that will end, I don't know. I guess we will see. Tomorrow I'll have a news conference and tell everyone that this is a cover up and that time travel is real. I have no idea what the fallout from that may be. I'll bet it is gonna be a bumpy ride," he said.

"I'm sure it will. The truth. That's an interesting approach. Not one I would have expected, but it does make a certain amount of sense. It will definitely improve access to the top scientists on the technology side of this thing," she said.

"Jonathan told me what William is up to. Did he tell you?" Robert asked.

"Yes. He said William wants to expose everything we do."

"That's what he told me. I have an opinion about what we should do. First, I want to hear what you think," he said.

"I think we should take him into our confidence. I think we

should have him take point on this with all the conspiracy theorists. He is deeper in that community than any of our other people. And I think we need to control what he tells the public. Either way we look at it, he will be exposing everything he knows. If we can give him what he wants, with controls on it, I think it will be a best case scenario," she said.

"That's it in a nutshell. I agree."

William walked past the slightly open door, pausing to look in cautiously. Robert did not see him. Sue did.

"Oh, William. Come in," Sue said.

He walked through the door. He fully understood what this meant. He knew what was coming. He had heard their conversations with Jonathan in the pit. Initially he thought about just taking what evidence he had and running. He knew he could disappear if he needed to. He had decided to wait and see just what Robert would be told. He knew he would have a chance to run if he felt it necessary. When he heard that the truth would be coming out, he decided to ride it out and see what Robert and Sue would do.

He expected just what he had heard from outside the door. The control they would use would be acceptable. They were going to do most of the work for him and he would have a much reduced exposure for himself. The danger he had anticipated he would encounter was now dissipated. Robert would be taking most of that on himself. William thought he could accept the situation. At least for the time being.

"What can I do for you?" William asked.

"We know you have been gathering information. Were you watching what was going on in the pit?" Robert asked.

"Yes. I heard everything. Let's not beat around the bush. I know you have a decision to make. I'll be a good soldier and play by the rules, if you really will come clean about what is in that pit. If you give me your word, I'll give you mine," William said.

"I think that will work. I give you my word that we will have the press conference tomorrow. I will tell the press there is no radon in the pit. I'll tell them that there is now evidence that time travel is possible and that the object in the pit is that evidence. We will release some of the photos and will have to deal with the fallout. Tomorrow will be an interesting day. Is that sufficient?" Robert said.

"I think so," William replied. He smiled a Robert and turned to

Sue. "Will you be able to explain this so that the press will be able to understand it?"

"I think so. I will have to be careful and make it clear that much of the technology that makes it possible does not yet exist. That is likely to be the biggest challenge."

"So what do you need from me?" William asked.

"Get me some of the best pictures of that thing that we have. I think after the press conference tomorrow you need to filter the information to some of the people you were going to give your evidence to. For now, the pictures and get your information organized. I'm sure there will be plenty to keep you busy after tomorrow. As for me, I need some coffee," Robert said.

Sue stood and said, "Me too."

"I'll get started," William said.

They left the room together. Sue and Robert headed toward the cafeteria. William went the other way, to the office where his eavesdropping computer was located.

Just inside the door of the little office, William stopped. This seemed strangely anticlimactic. He had worked his whole life trying to get to this point. Now it was time to move. Tomorrow would change it all. He was not sure how he felt about it. He was surprised to realize that he felt happy for perhaps the first time in years.

Chapter 61

"I'm ready," Hedwick said. Any resistance had been melted by Jonathan's simple demonstration.

"Good. First, let me ask you one more question. What would you be doing, if you were not in your present position?" Jonathan asked.

As totally unexpected as the question was, this was something Hedwick thought about often. She had spent many sleepless nights examining her life, wondering about where her path had diverged from her dreams.

Growing up, she had dreams of being a teacher. She had played school with her younger cousins, always as the teacher. She had worked as a tutor in college. She had loved the spark in the eyes of someone she was helping when she was able to get a difficult concept to make sense. That moment, when they finally "got it" was golden, precious. She had wanted to experience it everyday. Being a teacher, she had thought, would give her that. The other part of teaching for her had always been knowing a subject well enough to teach it. She had loved being a student as well. The "aha" moment she experienced when something complex clicked into place was almost as rewarding to her as seeing that moment in others. Her life had turned away from that, somehow. As things often do, her life had created transitions that had brought her to this place.

"I'd be a teacher," she said.

"Very good. That is what you will be doing. There are many things that are very complex which will require explanation in a way that lay people can understand. Sue understands what is going on here, on a deep technical level. But she will be too busy to take the time to translate that knowledge into a comprehensible whole so that a non-specialist can understand," Jonathan said.

"Who will I be teaching? I don't understand."

"Initially you will work closely with Sue, learning about the science, then you will work with Robert and Michelle on the public relations side of things. Essentially you will become a press secretary, the information specialist in all of this. Robert will be the figure head. You will handle the technical questions and relate to the press."

"For how long will that be my role? It doesn't sound too much like teaching."

"The first part, being the representative of this operation, will last a little over a year. Then the real teaching will begin. Tommy will be taking on a roll as a sort of evangelist to help bring about the understanding of the real impact of this event. He will talk about the freedom afforded by living in the knowledge that the future will happen a certain way. The freedom of knowing one's decisions are right with regard to the future, will liberate many people to be better than they might otherwise be. Tommy will be the figure head of that movement, but you will be the true teacher who helps masses of people understand the details and applications of that freedom."

"So I will be the next Mohamed, eh?" Hedwick asked. She smiled, not because she thought she was clever, but because she could see herself in the role being described to her. It was very appealing.

"Not exactly. This is not a religious movement per se. It also doesn't preclude religion. It simply states that it is okay to live by one's instincts, and to be guided by one's moral compass, and that the future will be what it will be as a result. There will be great challenges from religious leaders. Part of your role will be to teach them how this freedom does not mean that their own faith is in any way compromised. In fact you will actually help some of these leaders to strengthen their faith. Because once this projection disappears there will be no tangible evidence except these recordings, which will be challenged as being faked. You will have to help others to understand, by faith, that these things you have experienced are real. "You believe because you have seen, but you will need to help others believe who have not seen." This idea will actually make some religious leaders your greatest allies. At least those who truly understand what you are telling them. Others will oppose you, even after you make them understand. But you will make them understand, even if they do want not to believe you. That's all you can do.

"This is a lot to absorb. I will give you a few minutes to think, while you walk back and get Michelle and Tommy and Sue and

Robert. The last of what I have to say will concern all of you, so I will tell you together. Think while you walk, but go quickly and bring the others back with you."

"Alright...," Hedwick said. As she walked back toward the offices, her mind was numb for a moment. Then she felt almost giddy. She would get to be a teacher and see that awakening moment on the faces of others. She would get to be the true expert as well. She had always been a generalist in all she had done. The idea of being able to learn in depth and focus beyond her current understanding was very exciting.

Chapter 62

Hedwick became more excited as she walked back to the top of the quarry. She jogging by the time she reached the building. Michelle was just coming through the door as Hedwick approached.

Michelle was not sure if Hedwick saw her.

"Hello," Michelle said.

Hedwick was startled out of the daydream she was in. She had indeed not seen Michelle. She stopped short and gazed at her.

"Hello. Umm. Everyone is supposed to go out to the pit. Where are the others?" Hedwick asked.

"I'll get Tommy. I don't know where the other two are," Michelle said.

"Okay." Hedwick said. Obviously distracted, she walked into the building followed by Michelle.

Michelle wondered what had Hedwick so distracted. She also wondered if she would herself be as distracted after her trip to the pit. She went to the room where Tommy was lying. She watched him sleep. She made up her mind, in that moment, to try to build a relationship with him. She put no more on it than simply making the decision itself. She refused to think about the possibilities past the point of trying. It was all she could do. The future they faced was so uncertain. She could not be sure if there could be anything long term for them, truly for any of the people involved in this situation. Despite that, she felt she would rather face whatever was coming with Tommy, than alone.

"Tommy, wake up. It is time to go back to the pit."

He sat up and was fully awake almost instantly. "Alright, let's go." He was on his feet and headed toward the door. Michelle stood for a second and simply watched him. She was startled by how quickly he went from totally asleep to on the move. She followed him from the room.

Hedwick stopped at the office where she expected to find Robert. She was surprised to not find him there.

Robert had seen her walk past the door of the cafeteria and stepped into the hallway after she passed. He watched her as she stood at the door of the office. He thought briefly about ducking back into the cafeteria, or he could simply wait for her to turn around. He was enjoying looking at her. It made him think of their past times, when he had looked at her as more than a coworker. He wondered if those feelings would ever return. He wondered if those feelings he had felt were real and if she had ever cared for him.

She turned.

"There you are. We are all supposed to go back to the pit. Do you know where Sue is?"

"She is in the cafeteria with me," Robert answered automatically. His mind was still caught in the juxtaposition of past and future.

"Oh. Okay."

Looking at Hedwick, Robert was surprised by what he saw. Another juxtaposition presented itself. He saw a light in her eyes unlike anything he had ever seen. It seemed to take years from of her appearance. At the same time Robert saw the beginning of crow's feet at the corners of her eyes. Those he had not noticed before either. The multitude of thoughts passed through his mind in an instant. Then he returned to the moment.

"Are we ready?" Hedwick asked. At that moment Tommy and Michelle came into the hallway.

"Yes," Tommy said.

Without further discussion Robert turned and walked toward the pit. His thoughts returned to the light he had seen in Hedwick's eye. He did not doubt it was due to her encounter with Jonathan. He did wonder about the specifics of it. He knew he would find out the reason for the light soon enough.

The five headed toward the pit. Each of them silent. Each knowing they had been swept into something bigger and more important than themselves.

Chapter 63

"Welcome back to all of you." Jonathan said as they approached where he stood.

"I've spoken to those of you I needed to address alone. The rest of what I need to say is for all of you to hear. I will outline the entire plan for each of you. The biggest thing to remember during everything that is to come is to have faith that your decisions are the correct decisions. The fact I am here—I want to reinforce this—is sufficient evidence of that."

"Tommy. Now this comes to you. It is this fact, that our decisions will always be right, that will consume the rest of your life. You will be an evangelist of sorts. You will, with the help of Michelle and eventually Hedwick, spread this message. You will start soon, but not immediately. The next few weeks will be chaotic and your voice would be drowned out. After the first shock of what Robert and Michelle will set before the media begins to settle, then your work will begin.

"Michelle, initially you will help Robert with the press, reporting what is really going on here. I won't lie or sugar coat it. The next few weeks are going to be very difficult and dangerous. But know this, all of you will get through this. I cannot give you more details than that, but believe you will.

"To the specifics of where you will all begin: immediately after we are done here, Michelle and Robert will write the press release and prepare statements for the press conference to be held as soon as possible. Hedwick, you will need to get the press conference set up. Once you have made the arrangements, you will need to spend some time with Sue. You need to get a brief overview of the technical side of things. You will need to be up to speed at the press conference to answer a few questions. Sue, I'm sure you can help Hedwick with the basics. And I'm also sure you would like to write a quick draft of something to post on Arxiv to set precedence of the ideas we discussed when we spoke earlier. A brief outline of the idea only at this point, is all that you need to worry about. You will have the rest of your life to learn and expand all the details.

"And Tommy, you need to be seen at the press conference. But, don't speak. It is important for there to be no doubt of your pedigree when the time comes. It will be important for you to see the effect this news has on people in an unfiltered way, before it can be spun by the media. And be certain that there will be spin, both initially and in the long term."

"Tommy, stay with me a moment. The rest of you, please go and begin your tasks. This projection will be gone in only a few minutes more. Then the work will be left entirely to you."

Jonathan nodded as Robert, Hedwick, Sue and Michelle left. None of them doubted what they were to do. Michelle walked next to Robert and they began to discuss the best way to approach their statements and the press conference. Hedwick walked next to Sue and tried to find a common starting point to make the leap from her college, freshman physics to the complexity of what allowed a man in the future to project an image of himself into her present, his past.

"Tommy, I have two things I need to tell you, that are for you alone. Sue will be the only other person to know, and she will never tell. The message you will be spreading has nothing to do with religion. It is not about fate either. The future is and always has been determined by choices we make. Knowing that the future will work out to a certain point does not mean you are restricted. On the contrary, it means you can do what you think is right with absolute certainty that your decisions are the correct ones. They are the decisions that are consistent with the future that has already been assured by your past experiences. Bear in mind that doesn't mean there are no consequences to those decisions. It simply means that those decisions we each believe are right, lead to the future in which time travel is a reality.

Any time you have doubts about any of this, and there will be times, remember this. I am your grandson. You are the key to all of this."

"Now my time here is done. You must help others to have faith and then to act on that faith, even though there will no longer be any concrete evidence other than a few hours of recordings, that looks like it was produced in a movie studio. Stay strong, Grandpa." Jonathan said with a wry smile.

He turned and walked back to the black hole in the side of the object. A moment later there was brief flash, and the object was gone. There was no remaining trace of it.

Tommy sat on one of the rocks and laughed. Tears streamed from his eyes as the full implications of what he had just been told hit him. After a few minutes of reflection he headed toward the office building at the top of the pit.

Robert walked to the podium. He looked around the room He was more nervous than he had ever been at one of these things. He was also much more excited than he had ever been at a press conference.

He looked at Michelle, who was sitting in the front row. He had been amazed at the way she had put together his statement in a carefully worded way that would not allow for too much spin. It had also been her idea to play one of the reporters and serve up the first, prepared questions to which Robert had carefully prepared and rehearsed answers. She winked at him. He began.

"Ladies and gentlemen of the press. My name is Robert Braun. I am not a colonel in the Army. There is no radon in the quarry pit."

Visit
Second
Wind
Publishing

http://indigoseapress.com

www.ingramcontent.com/pod-product-compliance
Lightning Source LLC
Chambersburg PA
CBHW060437180626
46817CB00007B/2851